I0616720

A FOREGONE CONCLUSION

W. D. HOWELLS

1st WORLD
LIBRARY
Literary Society

A Foregone Conclusion

W. D. Howells

© 1st World Library, 2007
PO Box 2211
Fairfield, IA 52556
www.1stworldlibrary.com
First Edition

LCCN: 2007927875

Softcover ISBN: 978-1-4218-4575-3
Hardcover ISBN: 978-1-4218-4491-6
eBook ISBN: 978-1-4218-4659-0

Purchase *"A Foregone Conclusion"*
as a traditional bound book at:
www.1stWorldLibrary.com/purchase.asp?ISBN=978-1-4218-4575-3

1st World Library is a literary, educational organization
dedicated to:

- Creating a free internet library of downloadable ebooks

- Hosting writing competitions and offering book publishing
  scholarships.

Interested in more 1st World Library books? contact:
literacy@1stworldlibrary.com

Check us out at: www.1stworldlibrary.com

1ˢᵗ World Library Literary Society

Giving Back to the World

"If you want to work on the core problem, it's early school literacy."

- James Barksdale, former CEO of Netscape

"No skill is more crucial to the future of a child, or to a democratic and prosperous society, than literacy."

- Los Angeles Times

"Literacy... means far more than learning how to read and write... The aim is to transmit... knowledge and promote social participation."

- UNESCO

"Literacy is not a luxury, it is a right and a responsibility. If our world is to meet the challenges of the twenty-first century we must harness the energy and creativity of all our citizens."

- President Bill Clinton

"Parents should be encouraged to read to their children, and teachers should be equipped with all available techniques for teaching literacy, so the varying needs and capacities of individual kids can be taken into account."

- Hugh Mackay

I

As Don Ippolito passed down the long narrow *calle* or footway leading from the Campo San Stefano to the Grand Canal in Venice, he peered anxiously about him: now turning for a backward look up the calle, where there was no living thing in sight but a cat on a garden gate; now running a quick eye along the palace walls that rose vast on either hand and notched the slender strip of blue sky visible overhead with the lines of their jutting balconies, chimneys, and cornices; and now glancing toward the canal, where he could see the noiseless black boats meeting and passing. There was no sound in the calle save his own footfalls and the harsh scream of a parrot that hung in the sunshine in one of the loftiest windows; but the note of a peasant crying pots of pinks and roses in the campo came softened to Don Ippolito's sense, and he heard the gondoliers as they hoarsely jested together and gossiped, with the canal between them, at the next gondola station.

The first tenderness of spring was in the air though down in that calle there was yet enough of the wintry rawness to chill the tip of Don Ippolito's sensitive nose, which he rubbed for comfort with a handkerchief of dark blue calico, and polished for ornament with a handkerchief of white linen. He restored each to a different pocket in the sides of the ecclesiastical *talare*, or gown, reaching almost to his ankles, and then clutched the pocket in which he had replaced the linen handkerchief, as if to make sure that something he prized was safe within. He paused abruptly, and, looking at the doors he had passed, went back a few paces and stood before one over which hung, slightly tilted forward, an oval sign painted with the effigy of an eagle, a bundle of arrows, and certain thunderbolts, and bearing the legend, CONSULATE OF THE UNITED STATES, in neat characters. Don Ippolito gave a quick sigh, hesitated a moment, and then seized the bell-pull and jerked it so sharply that it seemed to thrust out, like a part of the mechanism, the head of an old serving-woman at the window above him.

"Who is there?" demanded this head.

"Friends," answered Don Ippolito in a rich, sad voice.

"And what do you command?" further asked the old woman.

Don Ippolito paused, apparently searching for his voice, before he inquired, "Is it here that the Consul of America lives?"

"Precisely."

"Is he perhaps at home?"

"I don't know. I will go ask him."

"Do me that pleasure, dear," said Don Ippolito, and remained knotting his fingers before the closed door. Presently the old woman returned, and looking out long enough to say, "The consul is at home," drew some inner bolt by a wire running to the lock, that let the door start open; then, waiting to hear Don Ippolito close it again, she called out from her height,

W. D. Howells

"Favor me above." He climbed the dim stairway to the point where she stood, and followed her to a door, which she flung open into an apartment so brightly lit by a window looking on the sunny canal, that he blinked as he entered. "Signor Console," said the old woman, "behold the gentleman who desired to see you;" and at the same time Don Ippolito, having removed his broad, stiff, three-cornered hat, came forward and made a beautiful bow. He had lost for the moment the trepidation which had marked his approach to the consulate, and bore himself with graceful dignity.

It was in the first year of the war, and from a motive of patriotism common at that time, Mr. Ferris (one of my many predecessors in office at Venice) had just been crossing his two silken gondola flags above the consular bookcase, where with their gilt lance-headed staves, and their vivid stars and stripes, they made a very pretty effect. He filliped a little dust from his coat, and begged Don Ippolito to be seated, with the air of putting even a Venetian priest on a footing of equality with other men under the folds of the national banner. Mr. Ferris had the prejudice of all Italian sympathizers against the priests; but for this he could hardly have found anything in Don Ippolito to alarm dislike. His face was a little thin, and the chin was delicate; the nose had a fine, Dantesque curve, but its final droop gave a melancholy cast to a countenance expressive of a gentle and kindly spirit; the eyes were large and dark and full of a dreamy warmth. Don Ippolito's prevailing tint was that transparent blueishness which comes from much shaving of a heavy black beard; his forehead and temples were marble white; he had a tonsure the size of a dollar. He sat silent for a little space, and softly questioned the consul's face with his dreamy eyes. Apparently he could not gather courage to speak of his business at once, for he turned his gaze upon the window and said, "A beautiful position, Signor Console."

"Yes, it's a pretty place," answered Mr. Ferris, warily.

"So much pleasanter here on the Canalazzo than on the campos or the little canals."

"Oh, without doubt."

"Here there must be constant amusement in watching the boats: great stir, great variety, great life. And now the fine season commences, and the Signor Console's countrymen will be coming to Venice. Perhaps," added Don Ippolito with a polite dismay, and an air of sudden anxiety to escape from his own purpose, "I may be disturbing or detaining the Signor Console?"

"No," said Mr. Ferris; "I am quite at leisure for the present. In what can I have the honor of serving you?"

Don Ippolito heaved a long, ineffectual sigh, and taking his linen handkerchief from his pocket, wiped his forehead with it, and rolled it upon his knee. He looked at the door, and all round the room, and then rose and drew near the consul, who had officially seated himself at his desk.

"I suppose that the Signor Console gives passports?" he asked.

"Sometimes," replied Mr. Ferris, with a clouding face.

Don Ippolito seemed to note the gathering distrust and to be helpless against it. He continued hastily: "Could the Signor Console give a passport for America ... to me?"

"Are you an American citizen?" demanded the consul in the voice of a man whose suspicions are fully roused.

"American citizen?"

"Yes; subject of the American republic."

"No, surely; I have not that happiness. I am an Austrian subject," returned Don Ippolito a little bitterly, as if the last words were an unpleasant morsel in the mouth.

"Then I can't give you a passport," said Mr. Ferris, somewhat more gently. "You know," he explained, "that no government can give passports to foreign subjects. That would be an unheard-of thing."

"But I thought that to go to America an American passport would be needed."

"In America," returned the consul, with proud compassion, "they don't care a fig for passports. You go and you come, and nobody meddles. To be sure," he faltered, "just now, on account of the secessionists, they *do* require you to show a passport at New York; but," he continued more boldly, "American passports are usually for Europe; and besides, all the American passports in the world wouldn't get *you* over the frontier at Peschiera. *You* must have a passport from the Austrian Lieutenancy of Venice,"

Don Ippolito nodded his head softly several times, and said, "Precisely," and then added with an indescribable weariness, "Patience! Signor Console, I ask your pardon for the trouble I have given," and he made the consul another low bow.

Whether Mr. Ferris's curiosity was piqued, and feeling himself on the safe side of his visitor he meant to know why he had come on such an errand, or whether he had some kindlier motive, he could hardly have told himself, but he said, "I'm very sorry. Perhaps there is something else in which I could be of use to you."

"Ah, I hardly know," cried Don Ippolito. "I really had a kind of hope in coming to your excellency."

"I am not an excellency," interrupted Mr. Ferris, conscientiously.

"Many excuses! But now it seems a mere bestiality. I was so ignorant about the other matter that doubtless I am also quite deluded in this."

"As to that, of course I can't say," answered Mr. Ferris, "but I hope not."

"Why, listen, signore!" said Don Ippolito, placing his hand over that pocket in which he kept his linen handkerchief. "I had something that it had come into my head to offer your honored government for its advantage in this deplorable rebellion."

"Oh," responded Mr. Ferris with a falling countenance. He had received so many offers of help for his honored government from sympathizing foreigners. Hardly a week passed but a sabre came clanking up his dim staircase with a Herr Graf or a Herr Baron attached, who appeared in the spotless panoply of his Austrian captaincy or lieutenancy, to accept from the consul a brigadier-generalship in the Federal armies, on condition that the consul would pay his expenses to Washington, or at least assure him of an exalted post and reimbursement of all outlays from President Lincoln as soon as he arrived. They were beautiful men, with the complexion of blonde girls; their uniforms fitted like kid gloves; the pale blue, or pure white, or huzzar black of their coats was ravishingly set off by their red or gold trimmings; and they were hard to make understand that brigadiers of American

W. D. Howells

birth swarmed at Washington, and that if they went thither, they must go as soldiers of fortune at their own risk. But they were very polite; they begged pardon when they knocked their scabbards against the consul's furniture, at the door they each made him a magnificent obeisance, said "Servus!" in their great voices, and were shown out by the old Marina, abhorrent of their uniforms and doubtful of the consul's political sympathies. Only yesterday she had called him up at an unwonted hour to receive the visit of a courtly gentleman who addressed him as Monsieur le Ministre, and offered him at a bargain ten thousand stand of probably obsolescent muskets belonging to the late Duke of Parma. Shabby, hungry, incapable exiles of all nations, religions, and politics beset him for places of honor and emolument in the service of the Union; revolutionists out of business, and the minions of banished despots, were alike willing to be fed, clothed, and dispatched to Washington with swords consecrated to the perpetuity of the republic.

"I have here," said Don Ippolito, too intent upon showing whatever it was he had to note the change in the consul's mood, "the model of a weapon of my contrivance, which I thought the government of the North could employ success-fully in cases where its batteries were in danger of capture by the Spaniards."

"Spaniards? Spaniards? We have no war with Spain!" cried the consul.

"Yes, yes, I know," Don Ippolito made haste to explain, "but those of South America being Spanish by descent"—

"But we are not fighting the South Americans. We are fighting our own Southern States, I am sorry to say."

"Oh! Many excuses. I am afraid I don't understand," said

Don Ippolito meekly; whereupon Mr. Ferris enlightened him in a formula (of which he was beginning to be weary) against European misconception of the American situation. Don Ippolito nodded his head contritely, and when Mr. Ferris had ended, he was so much abashed that he made no motion to show his invention till the other added, "But no matter; I suppose the contrivance would work as well against the Southerners as the South Americans. Let me see it, please;" and then Don Ippolito, with a gratified smile, drew from his pocket the neatly finished model of a breech-loading cannon.

"You perceive, Signor Console," he said with new dignity, "that this is nothing very new as a breech-loader, though I ask you to observe this little improvement for restoring the breech to its place, which is original. The grand feature of my invention, however, is this secret chamber in the breech, which is intended to hold an explosive of high potency, with a fuse coming out below. The gunner, finding his piece in danger, ignites this fuse, and takes refuge in flight. At the moment the enemy seizes the gun the contents of the secret chamber explode, demolishing the piece and destroying its captors."

The dreamy warmth in Don Ippolito's deep eyes kindled to a flame; a dark red glowed in his thin cheeks; he drew a box from the folds of his drapery and took snuff in a great whiff, as if inhaling the sulphurous fumes of battle, or titillating his nostrils with grains of gunpowder. He was at least in full enjoyment of the poetic power of his invention, and no doubt had before his eyes a vivid picture of a score of secessionists surprised and blown to atoms in the very moment of triumph. "Behold, Signor Console!" he said.

"It's certainly very curious," said Mr. Ferris, turning the fearful toy over in his hand, and admiring the neat workmanship of it. "Did you make this model yourself?"

"Surely," answered the priest, with a joyous pride; "I have no money to spend upon artisans; and besides, as you might infer, signore, I am not very well seen by my superiors and associates on account of these little amusements of mine; so keep them as much as I can to myself." Don Ippolito laughed nervously, and then fell silent with his eyes intent upon the consul's face. "What do you think, signore?" he presently resumed. "If this invention were brought to the notice of your generous government, would it not patronize my labors? I have read that America is the land of enterprises. Who knows but your government might invite me to take service under it in some capacity in which I could employ those little gifts that Heaven "—He paused again, apparently puzzled by the compassionate smile on the consul's lips." But tell me, signore, how this invention appears to you." "Have you had any practical experience in gunnery?" asked Mr. Ferris.

"Why, certainly not."

"Neither have I," continued Mr. Ferris, "but I was wondering whether the explosive in this secret chamber would not become so heated by the frequent discharges of the piece as to go off prematurely sometimes, and kill our own artillery-men instead of waiting for the secessionists?"

Don Ippolito's countenance fell, and a dull shame displaced the exultation that had glowed in it. His head sunk on his breast, and he made no attempt at reply, so that it was again Mr. Ferris who spoke. "You see, I don't really know anything more of the matter than you do, and I don't undertake to say whether your invention is disabled by the possibility I suggest or not. Haven't you any acquaintances among the military, to whom you could show your model?"

"No," answered Don Ippolito, coldly, "I don't consort with the military. Besides, what would be thought of a *priest*," he asked with a bitter stress on the word, "who exhibited such an invention as that to an officer of our paternal government?"

"I suppose it would certainly surprise the lieutenant-governor somewhat," said Mr. Ferris with a laugh. "May I ask," he pursued after an interval, "whether you have occupied yourself with other inventions?"

"I have attempted a great many," replied Don Ippolito in a tone of dejection.

"Are they all of this warlike temper?" pursued the consul.

"No," said Don Ippolito, blushing a little, "they are nearly all of peaceful intention. It was the wish to produce something of utility which set me about this cannon. Those good friends of mine who have done me the honor of looking at my attempts had blamed me for the uselessness of my inventions; they allowed that they were ingenious, but they said that even if they could be put in operation, they would not be what the world cared for. Perhaps they were right. I know very little of the world," concluded the priest, sadly. He had risen to go, yet seemed not quite able to do so; there was no more to say, but if he had come to the consul with high hopes, it might well have unnerved him to have all end so blankly. He drew a long, sibilant breath between his shut teeth, nodded to himself thrice, and turning to Mr. Ferris with a melancholy bow, said, "Signor Console, I thank you infinitely for your kindness, I beg your pardon for the disturbance, and I take my leave."

"I am sorry," said Mr. Ferris. "Let us see each other again. In regard to the inventions,—well, you must have patience." He dropped into some proverbial phrases which the obliging Latin tongues supply so abundantly for the races who must often talk when they do not feel like thinking, and he gave a start when Don Ippolito replied in English, "Yes, but hope deferred maketh the heart sick."

It was not that it was so uncommon to have Italians innocently come out with their whole slender stock of English to him, for the sake of practice, as they told him; but there were peculiarities in Don Ippolito's accent for which he could not account. "What," he exclaimed, "do you know English?"

"I have studied it a little, by my myself," answered Don Ippolito, pleased to have his English recognized, and then lapsing into the safety of Italian, he added, "And I had also the help of an English ecclesiastic who sojourned some months in Venice, last year, for his health, and who used to read with me and teach me the pronunciation. He was from Dublin, this ecclesiastic."

"Oh!" said Mr. Ferris, with relief, "I see;" and he perceived that what had puzzled him in Don Ippolito's English was a fine brogue superimposed upon his Italian accent.

"For some time I have had this idea of going to America, and I thought that the first thing to do was to equip myself with the language."

"Um!" said Mr. Ferris, "that was practical, at any rate," and he mused awhile. By and by he continued, more kindly than he had yet spoken, "I wish I could ask you to sit down again: but I have an engagement which I must make haste to keep. Are you going out through the campo? Pray wait a minute, and I will walk with you."

Mr. Ferris went into another room, through the open door of which Don Ippolito saw the paraphernalia of a painter's studio: an easel with a half-finished picture on it; a chair with a palette and brushes, and crushed and twisted tubes of colors; a lay figure in one corner; on the walls scraps of stamped leather, rags of tapestry, desultory sketches on paper.

Mr. Ferris came out again, brushing his hat.

"The Signor Console amuses himself with painting, I see," said Don Ippolito courteously.

"Not at all," replied Mr. Ferris, putting on his gloves; "I am a painter by profession, and I amuse myself with consuling;" [Footnote: Since these words of Mr. Ferris were first printed, I have been told that a more eminent painter, namely Rubens, made very much the same reply to very much the same remark, when Spanish Ambassador in England. "The Ambassador of His Catholic Majesty, I see, amuses himself by painting sometimes," said a visitor who found him at his easel. "I amuse myself by playing the ambassador sometimes," answered Rubens. In spite of the similarity of the speeches, I let that of Mr. Ferris stand, for I am satisfied that he did not know how unhandsomely Rubens had taken the words out of his mouth.] and as so open a matter needed no explanation, he said no more about it. Nor is it quite necessary to tell how, as he was one day painting in New York, it occurred to him to make use of a Congressional friend, and ask for some Italian consulate, he did not care which. That of Venice happened to be vacant: the income was a few hundred dollars; as no one else wanted it, no question was made of Mr. Ferris's fitness for the post, and he presently found himself possessed of a commission requesting the Emperor of Austria to permit him to enjoy and exercise the office of consul of the ports of the Lombardo-Venetian kingdom, to which the President of the United States appointed him from a special trust in his abilities and integrity. He proceeded at once to his post of duty, called upon the ship's chandler with whom they had been left, for the consular archives, and began to paint some Venetian subjects.

He and Don Ippolito quitted the Consulate together, leaving Marina to digest with her noonday porridge the wonder that he should be walking amicably forth with a priest. The same spectacle was presented to the gaze of the campo, where they paused in friendly converse, and were seen to part with many politenesses by the doctors of the neighborhood, lounging away their leisure, as the Venetian fashion is, at the local pharmacy.

The apothecary craned forward over his counter, and peered through the open door. "What is that blessed Consul of America doing with a priest?"

"The Consul of America with a priest?" demanded a grave old man, a physician with a beautiful silvery beard, and a most reverend and senatorial presence, but one of the worst tongues in Venice. "Oh!" he added, with a laugh, after scrutiny of the two through his glasses, "it's that crack-brain Don Ippolito Rondinelli. He isn't priest enough to hurt the consul. Perhaps he's been selling him a perpetual motion for the use of his government, which needs something of the kind just now. Or maybe he's been posing to him for a picture. He would make a very pretty Joseph, give him Potiphar's wife in the background," said the doctor, who if not maligned would have needed much more to make a Joseph of him.

II

Mr. Ferris took his way through the devious footways where the shadow was chill, and through the broad campos where the sun was tenderly warm, and the towers of the church rose against the speck-less azure of the vernal heaven. As he went along, he frowned in a helpless perplexity with the case of Don Ippolito, whom he had begun by doubting for a spy with some incomprehensible motive, and had ended by pitying with a certain degree of amusement and a deep sense of the futility of his compassion. He presently began to think of him with a little disgust, as people commonly think of one whom they pity and yet cannot help, and he made haste to cast off the hopeless burden. He shrugged his shoulders, struck his stick on the smooth paving-stones, and let his eyes rove up and down the fronts of the houses, for the sake of the pretty faces that glanced out of the casements. He was a young man, and it was spring, and this was Venice. He made himself joyfully part of the city and the season; he was glad of the narrowness of the streets, of the good-humored jostling and pushing; he crouched into an arched doorway to let a water-carrier pass with her copper buckets dripping at the end of the yoke balanced on her shoulder, and he returned her smiles and excuses with others as broad and gay; he brushed by the swelling hoops of ladies, and stooped before the unwieldy burdens of porters, who as they staggered through the crowd with a thrust hero, and a shove there forgave themselves, laughing, with "We are in Venice, signori;" and he stood aside for the files of soldiers clanking heavily over the pavement, then muskets kindling to a blaze in the sunlit campos and quenched again in the damp shadows of the calles. His ear was taken by the vibrant jargoning of the boatmen as they pushed their craft under the bridges he crossed, and the keen notes of the canaries and the songs of the golden-billed blackbirds whose cages hung at lattices far overhead. Heaps of oranges, topped by the fairest cut in halves, gave their color, at frequent intervals, to the dusky corners and recesses and the long-drawn cry of the venders, "Oranges of Palermo!" rose above the clatter of feet and the clamor of other voices. At a little shop where butter and eggs and milk abounded, together with early flowers of various sorts, he bought a bunch of hyacinths, blue and white and yellow, and he presently stood smelling these while he waited in the hotel parlor for the ladies to whom he had sent his card. He turned at the sound of drifting drapery, and could not forbear placing the hyacinths in the hand of Miss Florida Vervain, who had come into the room to receive him. She was a girl of about seventeen years, who looked older; she was tall rather than short, and rather full,—though it could not be said that she erred in point of solidity. In the attitudes of shy hauteur into which she constantly fell, there was a touch of defiant awkwardness which had a certain fascination. She was blonde, with a throat and hands of milky whiteness; there was a suggestion of freckles on her regular face, where a quick color came and went, though her cheeks were habitually somewhat pale; her eyes were very blue under their level brows, and the lashes were even lighter in color than the masses of her fair gold hair; the edges of the lids were touched with the faintest red. The late Colonel Vervain of the United States army, whose complexion his daughter had inherited, was an officer whom it would not have been peaceable to cross in any purpose or pleasure, and Miss Vervain seemed sometimes a little burdened by the passionate nature which he had left her together with the tropical name he had bestowed in honor of the State where he had fought the Seminoles in his youth, and where he chanced still to be stationed when she was born; she had the air of being embarrassed in presence of herself, and of having an anxious watch upon her impulses. I do not know how otherwise to describe the effort of proud, helpless femininity, which would have struck the close observer in Miss Vervain.

"Delicious!" she said, in a deep voice, which conveyed something of this anxiety in its guarded tones, and yet was not wanting in a kind of frankness. "Did you mean them for me, Mr. Ferris?"

"I didn't, but I do," answered Mr. Ferris. "I bought them in ignorance, but I understand now what they were meant for by nature;" and in fact the hyacinths, with their smooth textures and their pure colors, harmonized well with Miss Vervain, as she bent her face over them and inhaled their full, rich perfume.

"I will put them in water," she said, "if you'll excuse me a moment. Mother will be down directly."

Before she could return, her mother rustled into the parlor.

Mrs. Vervain was gracefully, fragilely unlike her daughter. She entered with a gentle and gliding step, peering near-sightedly about through her glasses, and laughing triumphantly when she had determined Mr. Ferris's exact position, where he stood with a smile shaping his full brown beard and glancing from his hazel eyes. She was dressed in perfect taste with reference to her matronly years, and the lingering evidences of her widowhood, and she had an unaffected naturalness of manner which even at her age of forty-eight could not be called less than charming. She spoke in a trusting, caressing tone, to which no man at least could respond unkindly.

"So very good of you, to take all this trouble, Mr. Ferris," she said, giving him a friendly hand, "and I suppose you are letting us encroach upon very valuable time. I'm quite ashamed to take it. But isn't it a heavenly day? What *I* call a perfect day, just right every way; none of those disagreeable extremes. It's so unpleasant to have it too hot, for instance. I'm the greatest person for moderation, Mr. Ferris, and I carry the principle into everything; but I do think the breakfasts at these Italian hotels are too light altogether. I like our American breakfasts, don't you? I've been telling Florida I can't stand it; we really must make some arrangement. To be sure, you oughtn't to think of such a thing as eating, in a place like Venice, all poetry; but a sound mind in a sound body, *I* say. We're perfectly wild over it. Don't you think it's a place that grows upon you very much, Mr. Ferris? All those associations,—it does seem too much; and the gondolas everywhere. But I'm always afraid the gondoliers cheat us; and in the stores I never feel safe a moment—not a moment. I do think the Venetians are lacking in truthfulness, a little. I don't believe they understand our American fairdealing and sincerity. I shouldn't want to do them injustice, but I really think they take advantages in bargaining. Now such a thing even as corals. Florida is extremely fond of them, and we bought a set yesterday in the Piazza, and I *know* we paid too much for them. Florida," said Mrs. Vervain, for her daughter had reentered the room, and stood with some shawls and wraps upon her arm, patiently waiting for the conclusion of the elder lady's speech, "I wish you would bring down that set of corals. I'd like Mr. Ferris to give an unbiased opinion. I'm sure we were cheated."

"I don't know anything about corals, Mrs. Vervain,"

interposed Mr. Ferris.

"Well, but you ought to see this set for the beauty of the color; they're really exquisite. I'm sure it will gratify your artistic taste."

Miss Vervain hesitated with a look of desire to obey, and of doubt whether to force the pleasure upon Mr. Ferris. "Won't it do another time, mother?" she asked faintly; "the gondola is waiting for us."

Mrs. Vervain gave a frailish start from the chair, into which she had sunk, "Oh, do let us be off at once, then," she said; and when they stood on the landing-stairs of the hotel: "What gloomy things these gondolas are!" she added, while the gondolier with one foot on the gunwale of the boat received the ladies' shawls, and then crooked his arm for them to rest a hand on in stepping aboard; "I wonder they don't paint them some cheerful color."

"Blue, or pink, Mrs. Vervain?" asked Mr. Ferris. "I knew you were coming to that question; they all do. But we needn't have the top on at all, if it depresses your spirits. We shall be just warm enough in the open sunlight."

"Well, have it off, then. It sends the cold chills over me to look at it. What *did* Byron call it?"

"Yes, it's time for. Byron, now. It was very good of you not to mention him before, Mrs. Vervain. Bat I knew he had to come. He called it a coffin clapped in a canoe."

"Exactly," said Mrs. Vervain. "I always feel as if I were going to my own funeral when I get into it; and I've certainly had enough of funerals never to want to have anything to do with another, as long as I live."

She settled herself luxuriously upon the feather-stuffed leathern cushions when the cabin was removed. Death had indeed been near her very often; father and mother had been early lost to her, and the brothers and sisters orphaned with her had faded and perished one after another, as they ripened to men and women; she had seen four of her own children die; her husband had been dead six years. All these bereavements had left her what they had found her. She had truly grieved, and, as she said, she had hardly ever been out of black since she could remember.

"I never was in colors when I was a girl," she went on, indulging many obituary memories as the gondola dipped and darted down the canal, "and I was married in my mourning for my last sister. It did seem a little too much when she went, Mr. Ferris. I was too young to feel it so much about the others, but we were nearly of the same age, and that makes a difference, don't you know. First a brother and then a sister: it was very strange how they kept going that way. I seemed to break the charm when I got married; though, to be sure, there was no brother left after Marian."

Miss Vervain heard her mother's mortuary prattle with a face from which no impatience of it could be inferred, and Mr. Ferris made no comment on what was oddly various in character and manner, for Mrs. Vervain touched upon the gloomiest facts of her history with a certain impersonal statistical interest. They were rowing across the lagoon to the Island of San Lazzaro, where for reasons of her own she intended to venerate the convent in which Byron studied the Armenian language preparatory to writing his great poem in it; if her pilgrimage had no very earnest motive, it was worthy of the fact which it was designed to honor. The lagoon was of a perfect, shining smoothness, broken by the shallows over which the ebbing tide had left the sea-weed trailed like long, disheveled hair. The fishermen, as they waded about staking their nets, or stooped to gather the small shell-fish of the shallows, showed legs as brown and tough as those of the apostles in Titian's Assumption. Here and there was a boat, with a boy or an old man asleep in the bottom of it. The gulls sailed high, white flakes against the illimitable blue of the heavens; the air, though it was of early spring, and in the shade had a salty pungency, was here almost languorously warm; in the motionless splendors and rich colors of the scene there was a melancholy before which Mrs. Vervain fell fitfully silent. Now and then Ferris briefly spoke, calling Miss Vervain's notice to this or that, and she briefly responded. As they passed the mad-house of San Servolo, a maniac standing at an open window took his black velvet skull-cap from his white hair, bowed low three times, and kissed his hand to the ladies. The Lido in front of them stretched a brown strip of sand with white villages shining out of it; on their left the Public Gardens showed a mass of hovering green; far beyond and above, the ghostlike snows of the Alpine heights haunted the misty horizon.

It was chill in the shadow of the convent when they landed at San Lazzaro, and it was cool in the parlor where they waited for the monk who was to show them through the place; but it was still and warm in the gardened court, where the bees murmured among the crocuses and hyacinths under the noonday sun. Miss Vervain stood looking out of the window upon the lagoon, while her mother drifted about the room, peering at the objects on the wall through her eyeglasses. She was praising a Chinese painting of fish on rice-paper, when a young monk entered with a cordial greeting in English for Mr. Ferris. She turned and saw them shaking hands, but at the same moment her eyeglasses abandoned her nose with a vigorous leap; she gave an amiable laugh, and groping for them over her dress, bowed at random as Mr. Ferris presented Padre Girolamo.

"I've been admiring this painting so much, Padre Girolamo," she said, with instant good-will, and taking the monk into the easy familiarity of her friendship by the tone with which she spoke his name. "Some of the brothers did it, I suppose."

"Oh no," said the monk, "it's a Chinese painting. We hung it up there because it was given to us, and was curious."

"Well, now, do you know," returned Mrs. Vervain, "I *thought* it was Chinese! Their things *are*, so odd. But really, in an Armenian convent it's very misleading. I don't think you ought to leave it there; it certainly does throw people off the track," she added, subduing the expression to something very lady-like, by the winning appeal with which she used it.

"Oh, but if they put up Armenian paintings in Chinese convents?" said Mr. Ferris.

"You're joking!" cried Mrs. Vervain, looking at him with a graciously amused air. "There *are* no Chinese convents. To be sure those rebels are a kind of Christians," she added thoughtfully, "but there can't be many of them left, poor things, hundreds of them executed at a time, that way. It's perfectly sickening to read of it; and you can't help it, you know. But they say they haven't really so much feeling as we have—not so nervous."

She walked by the side of the young friar as he led the way to such parts of the convent as are open to visitors, and Mr. Ferris came after with her daughter, who, he fancied, met his attempts at talk with sudden and more than usual hauteur. "What a fool!" he said to himself. "Is she afraid I shall be wanting to make love to her?" and he followed in rather a sulky silence the course of Mrs. Vervain and her guide. The library, the chapel, and the museum called out her friendliest praises, and in the last she praised the mummy on show there at the expense of one she had seen in New York; but when Padre Girolamo pointed out the desk in the refectory from which one of the brothers read while the rest were eating, she took him to task. "Oh, but I can't think that's at all good for the digestion, you know,—using the brain that way whilst you're at table. I really hope you don't listen too attentively; it would be better for you in the long run, even in a religious point of view. But now—Byron! You *must* show me his cell!" The monk deprecated the non-existence of such a cell, and glanced in perplexity at Mr. Ferris, who came to his relief. "You couldn't have seen his cell, if he'd had one, Mrs. Vervain. They don't admit ladies to the cloister."

"What nonsense!" answered Mrs. Vervain, apparently regarding this as another of Mr. Ferris's pleasantries; but Padre Girolamo silently confirmed his statement, and she briskly assailed the rule as a disrespect to the sex, which reflected even upon the Virgin, the object, as he was forced to allow, of their high veneration. He smiled patiently, and confessed that Mrs. Vervain had all the reasons on her side. At the polyglot printing-office, where she handsomely bought every kind of Armenian book and pamphlet, and thus repaid in the only way possible the trouble their visit had given, he did not offer to take leave of them, but after speaking with Ferris, of whom he seemed an old friend, he led them through the garden environing the convent, to a little pavilion perched on the wall that defends the island from the tides of the lagoon. A lay-brother presently followed them, bearing a tray with coffee, toasted rusk, and a jar of that conserve of rose-leaves which is the convent's delicate hospitality to favored guests. Mrs. Vervain cried out over the poetic confection when Padre Girolamo told her what it was, and her daughter suffered herself to express a guarded pleasure. The amiable matron brushed the crumbs of the *baicolo* from her lap when the lunch was ended, and fitting on her glasses leaned forward for a better look at the monk's black-bearded face.

"I'm perfectly delighted," she said. "You must be very happy here. I suppose you are."

"Yes," answered the monk rapturously; "so happy that I should be content never to leave San Lazzaro. I came here when I was very young, and the greater part of my life has been passed on this little island. It is my home—my country."

"Do you never go away?"

"Oh yes; sometimes to Constantinople, sometimes to London and Paris."

"And you've never been to America yet? Well now, I'll tell you; you ought to go. You would like it, I know, and our people would give you a very cordial reception."

"Reception?" The monk appealed once more to Ferris with a look.

Ferris broke into a laugh. "I don't believe Padre Girolamo would come in quality of distinguished foreigner, Mrs. Vervain, and I don't think he'd know what to do with one of our cordial receptions."

"Well, he ought to go to America, any way. He can't really know anything about us till he's been there. Just think how ignorant the English are of our country! You *will* come, won't you? I should be delighted to welcome you at my house in Providence. Rhode Island is a small State, but there's a great deal of wealth there, and very good society in Providence. It's quite New-Yorky, you know," said Mrs. Vervain expressively. She rose as she spoke, and led the way back to the gondola. She told Padre Girolamo that they were to be some weeks in Venice, and made him promise to breakfast with them at their hotel. She smiled and nodded to him after the boat had pushed off, and kept him bowing on the landing-stairs.

"What a lovely place, and what a perfectly heavenly morning you *have* given us, Mr. Ferris I We never can thank you enough for it. And now, do you know what I'm thinking of? Perhaps you can help me. It was Byron's studying there put me in mind of it. How soon do the mosquitoes come?"

"About the end of June," responded Ferris mechanically, staring with helpless mystification at Mrs. Vervain.

"Very well; then there's no reason why we shouldn't stay in Venice till that time. We are both very fond of the place, and we'd quite concluded, this morning, to stop here till the mosquitoes came. You know, Mr. Ferris, my daughter had to leave school much earlier than she ought, for my health has obliged me to travel a great deal since I lost my husband; and I must have her with me, for we're all that there is of us; we haven't a chick or a child that's related to us anywhere. But wherever we stop, even for a few weeks, I contrive to get her some kind of instruction. I feel the need of it so much in my own case; for to tell you the truth, Mr. Ferris, I married too young. I suppose I should do the same thing over again if it was to be done over; but don't you see, my mind wasn't properly formed; and then following my husband about from pillar to post, and my first baby born when I was nineteen— well, it wasn't education, at any rate, whatever else it was; and I've determined that Florida, though we are such a pair of wanderers, shall not have my regrets. I got teachers for her in England,—the English are not anything like so disagreeable at home as they are in traveling, and we stayed there two years,—and I did in France, and I did in Germany. And now, Italian. Here we are in Italy, and I think we ought to improve the time. Florida knows a good deal of Italian already, for her music teacher in France was an Italian, and he taught her the language as well as music. What she wants now, I should say, is to perfect her accent and get facility. I think she ought to have some one come every day and read and converse an hour or two with her."

Mrs. Vervain leaned back in her seat, and looked at Ferris, who said, feeling that the matter was referred to him, "I think—without presuming to say what Miss Vervain's need of instruction is—that your idea is a very good one." He mused in silence his wonder that so much addlepatedness as was at once observable in Mrs. Vervain should exist along with so much common-sense. "It's certainly very good in the abstract," he added, with a glance at the daughter, as if the sense must be hers. She did not meet his glance at once, but with an impatient recognition of the heat that was now great for the warmth with which she was dressed, she pushed her sleeve from her wrist, showing its delicious whiteness, and letting her fingers trail through the cool water; she dried them on her handkerchief, and then bent her eyes full upon him as if challenging him to think this unlady-like.

"No, clearly the sense does not come from her," said Ferris to himself; it is impossible to think well of the mind of a girl who treats one with tacit contempt.

"Yes," resumed Mrs. Vervain, "it's certainly very good in the abstract. But oh dear me! you've no idea of the difficulties in the way. I may speak frankly with you, Mr. Ferris, for you are here as the representative of the country, and you naturally sympathize with the difficulties of Americans abroad; the teachers will fall in love with their pupils."

"Mother!" began Miss Vervain; and then she checked herself.

Ferris gave a vengeful laugh. "Really, Mrs. Vervain, though I sympathize with you in my official capacity, I must own that as a man and a brother, I can't help feeling a little sorry for those poor fellows, too."

"To be sure, they are to be pitied, of course, and *I* feel for them; I did when I was a girl; for the same thing used to happen then. I don't know why Florida should be subjected to such embarrassments, too. It does seem sometimes as if it were something in the blood. They all get the idea that you have money, you know."

"Then I should say that it might be something in the pocket," suggested Ferris with a look at Miss Vervain, in whose silent suffering, as he imagined it, he found a malicious consolation for her scorn.

"Well, whatever it is," replied Mrs. Vervain, "it's too vexatious. Of course, going to new places, that way, as we're always doing, and only going to stay for a limited time, perhaps, you can't pick and choose. And even when you *do* get an elderly teacher, they're as bad as any. It really is too trying. Now, when I was talking with that nice monk of yours at the convent, there, I couldn't help thinking how perfectly delightful it would be if Florida could have *him* for a teacher. Why couldn't she? He told me that he would come to take breakfast or lunch with us, but not dinner, for he always had to be at the convent before nightfall. Well, he might come to give the lessons sometime in the middle of the day."

"You couldn't manage it, Mrs. Vervain, I know you couldn't," answered Ferris earnestly. "I'm sure the Armenians never do anything of the kind. They're all very busy men, engaged in ecclesiastical or literary work, and they couldn't give the time."

"Why not? There was Byron."

"But Byron went to them, and he studied Armenian, not Italian, with them. Padre Girolamo speaks perfect Italian, for all that I can see; but I doubt if he'd undertake to impart the native accent, which is what you want. In fact, the scheme is altogether impracticable."

"Well," said Mrs. Vervain; "I'm exceedingly sorry. I had quite set my heart on it. I never took such a fancy to any one in such a short time before."

"It seemed to be a case of love at first sight on both sides," said Ferris. "Padre Girolamo doesn't shower those syruped rose-leaves indiscriminately upon visitors."

"Thanks," returned Mrs. Vervain; "it's very good of you to say so, Mr. Ferris, and it's very gratifying, all round; but don't you see, it doesn't serve the present purpose. What teachers do you know of?"

She had been by marriage so long in the service of the United States that she still regarded its agents as part of her own domestic economy. Consuls she everywhere employed as functionaries specially appointed to look after the interests of American ladies traveling without protection. In the week which had passed since her arrival in Venice, there had been no day on which she did not appeal to Ferris for help or sympathy or advice. She took amiable possession of him at once, and she had established an amusing sort of intimacy with him, to which the haughty trepidations of her daughter set certain bounds, but in which the demand that he should find her a suitable Italian teacher seemed trivially matter of course.

"Yes. I know several teachers," he said, after thinking

awhile; "but they're all open to the objection of being human; and besides, they all do things in a set kind of way, and I'm afraid they wouldn't enter into the spirit of any scheme of instruction that departed very widely from Ollendorff." He paused, and Mrs. Vervain gave a sketch of the different professional masters whom she had employed in the various countries of her sojourn, and a disquisition upon their several lives and characters, fortifying her statements by reference of doubtful points to her daughter. This occupied some time, and Ferris listened to it all with an abstracted air. At last he said, with a smile, "There was an Italian priest came to see me this morning, who astonished me by knowing English—with a brogue that he'd learned from an English priest straight from Dublin; perhaps *he* might do, Mrs. Vervain? He's professionally pledged, you know, not to give the kind of annoyance you've suffered from in teachers. He would do as well as Padre Girolamo, I suppose."

"Do you really? Are you in earnest?"

"Well, no, I believe I'm not. I haven't the least idea he would do. He belongs to the church militant. He came to me with the model of a breech-loading cannon he's invented, and he wanted a passport to go to America, so that he might offer his cannon to our government."

"How curious!" said Mrs. Vervain, and her daughter looked frankly into Ferris's face. "But I know; it's one of your jokes."

"You overpraise me, Mrs. Vervain. If I could make such jokes as that priest was, I should set up for a humorist at once. He had the touch of pathos that they say all true pieces of humor ought to have," he went on instinctively addressing himself to Miss Vervain, who did not repulse him. "He made me melancholy; and his face haunts me. I should like to paint him. Priests are generally such a snuffy, common lot. And I dare say," he concluded, "he's sufficiently commonplace, too, though he didn't look it. Spare your romance, Miss Vervain."

The young lady blushed resentfully. "I see as little romance as joke in it," she said.

"It was a cannon," returned Ferris, without taking any notice of her, and with a sort of absent laugh, "that would make it very lively for the Southerners—if they had it. Poor fellow! I suppose he came with high hopes of me, and expected me to receive his invention with eloquent praises. I've no doubt he figured himself furnished not only with a passport, but with a letter from me to President Lincoln, and foresaw his own triumphal entry into Washington, and his honorable interviews with the admiring generals of the Union forces, to whom he should display his wonderful cannon. Too bad; isn't it?"

"And why didn't you give him the passport and the letter?" asked Mrs. Vervain.

"Oh, that's a state secret," returned Ferris.

"And you think he won't do for our purpose?"

"I don't indeed."

"Well, I'm not so sure of it. Tell me something more about him."

"I don't know anything more about him. Besides, there isn't time."

The gondola had already entered the canal, and was swiftly

approaching the hotel.

"Oh yes, there is," pleaded Mrs. Vervain, laying her hand on his arm. "I want you to come in and dine with us. We dine early."

"Thank you, I can't. Affairs of the nation, you know. Rebel privateer on the canal of the Brenta."

"Really?" Mrs. Vervain leaned towards Ferris for sharper scrutiny of his face. Her glasses sprang from her nose, and precipitated themselves into his bosom.

"Allow me," he said, with burlesque politeness, withdrawing them from the recesses of his waistcoat and gravely presenting them. Miss Vervain burst into a helpless laugh; then she turned toward her mother with a kind of indignant tenderness, and gently arranged her shawl so that it should not drop off when she rose to leave the gondola. She did not look again at Ferris, who resisted Mrs. Vervain's entreaties to remain, and took leave as soon as the gondola landed.

The ladies went to their room, where Florida lifted from the table a vase of divers-colored hyacinths, and stepping out upon the balcony flung the flowers into the canal. As she put down the empty vase, the lingering perfume of the banished flowers haunted the air of the room.

"Why, Florida," said her mother, "those were the flowers that Mr. Ferris gave you. Did you fancy they had begun to decay? The smell of hyacinths when they're a little old is dreadful. But I can't imagine a gentleman's giving you flowers that were at all old."

"Oh, mother, don't speak to me!" cried Miss Vervain, passionately, clasping her hands to her face.

"Now I see that I've been saying something to vex you, my darling," and seating herself beside the young girl on the sofa, she fondly took down her hands. "Do tell me what it was. Was it about your teachers falling in love with you? You know they did, Florida: Pestachiavi and Schulze, both; and that horrid old Fleuron."

"Did you think I liked any better on that account to have you talk it over with a stranger?" asked Florida, still angrily.

"That's true, my dear," said Mrs. Vervain, penitently. "But if it worried you, why didn't you do something to stop me? Give me a hint, or just a little knock, somewhere?"

"No, mother; I'd rather not. Then you'd have come out with the whole thing, to prove that you were right. It's better to let it go," said Florida with a fierce laugh, half sob. "But it's strange that you can't remember how such things torment me."

"I suppose it's my weak health, dear," answered the mother. "I didn't use to be so. But now I don't really seem to have the strength to be sensible. I know it's silly as well as you. The talk just seems to keep going on of itself,—slipping out, slipping out. But you needn't mind. Mr. Ferris won't think you could ever have done anything out of the way. I'm sure you don't act with *him* as if you'd ever encouraged anybody. I think you're too haughty with him, Florida. And now, his flowers."

"He's detestable. He's conceited and presuming beyond all endurance. I don't care what he thinks of me. But it's his manner towards you that I can't tolerate."

"I suppose it's rather free," said Mrs. Vervain. "But then you know, my dear, I shall be soon getting to be an old lady; and besides, I always feel as if consuls were a kind of one of the family. He's been very obliging since we came; I don't know what we should have done without him. And I don't object to a little ease of manner in the gentlemen; I never did."

"He makes fun of you," cried Florida: "and there at the convent,", she said, bursting into angry tears, "he kept exchanging glances with that monk as if he.... He's insulting, and I hate him!"

"Do you mean that he thought your mother ridiculous, Florida?" asked Mrs. Vervain gravely. "You must have misunderstood his looks; indeed you must. I can't imagine why he should. I remember that I talked particularly well during our whole visit; my mind was active, for I felt unusually strong, and I was interested in everything. It's nothing but a fancy of yours; or your prejudice, Florida. But it's odd, now I've sat down for a moment, how worn out I feel. And thirsty."

Mrs. Vervain fitted on her glasses, but even then felt uncertainly about for the empty vase on the table before her.

"It isn't a goblet, mother," said Florida; "I'll get you some water."

"Do; and then throw a shawl over me. I'm sleepy, and a nap before dinner will do me good. I don't see why I'm so drowsy of late. I suppose it's getting into the sea air here at Venice; though it's mountain air that makes you drowsy. But you're quite mistaken about Mr. Ferris. He isn't capable of anything really rude. Besides, there wouldn't have been any sense in it."

The young girl brought the water and then knelt beside the sofa, on which she arranged the pillows under her mother,

W. D. Howells

and covered her with soft wraps. She laid her cheek against the thinner face. "Don't mind anything I've said, mother; let's talk of something else."

The mother drew some loose threads of the daughter's hair through her slender fingers, but said little more, and presently fell into a deep slumber. Florida gently lifted her head away, and remained kneeling before the sofa, looking into the sleeping face with an expression of strenuous, compassionate devotion, mixed with a vague alarm and self-pity, and a certain wondering anxiety.

III

Don Ippolito had slept upon his interview with Ferris, and now sat in his laboratory, amidst the many witnesses of his inventive industry, with the model of the breech-loading cannon on the workbench before him. He had neatly mounted it on wheels, that its completeness might do him the greater credit with the consul when he should show it him, but the carriage had been broken in his pocket, on the way home, by an unlucky thrust from the burden of a porter, and the poor toy lay there disabled, as if to dramatize that premature explosion in the secret chamber.

His heart was in these inventions of his, which had as yet so grudgingly repaid his affection. For their sake he had stinted himself of many needful things. The meagre stipend which he received from the patrimony of his church, eked out with the money paid him for baptisms, funerals, and marriages, and for masses by people who had friends to be prayed out of purgatory, would at best have barely sufficed to support him; but he denied himself everything save the necessary decorums of dress and lodging; he fasted like a saint, and slept hard as a hermit, that he might spend upon these ungrateful creatures of his brain. They were the work of his own hands, and so he saved the expense of their construction; but there were many little outlays for materials and for tools, which he could not avoid, and with him a little was all. They not only famished him; they isolated him. His superiors in the church, and his brother priests, looked with doubt or ridicule upon the labors for which he shunned their company, while he gave up the other social joys, few and small, which a priest might know in the Venice of that day, when all generous spirits regarded him with suspicion for his cloth's sake, and church and state were alert to detect disaffection or indifference in him. But bearing these things willingly, and living as frugally as he might, he had still not enough, and he had been fain to assume the instruction of a young girl of old and noble family in certain branches of polite learning which a young lady of that sort might fitly know. The family was not so rich as it was old and noble, and Don Ippolito was paid from its purse rather than its pride. But the slender salary was a help; these patricians were very good to him; many a time he dined with them, and so spared the cost of his own pottage at home; they always gave him coffee when he came, and that was a saving; at the proper seasons little presents from them were not wanting. In a word, his condition was not privation. He did his duty as a teacher faithfully, and the only trouble with it was that the young girl was growing into a young woman, and that he could not go on teaching her forever. In an evil hour, as it seemed to Don Ippolito, that made the years she had been his pupil shrivel to a mere pinch of time, there came from a young count of the Friuli, visiting Venice, an offer of marriage; and Don Ippolito lost his place. It was hard, but he bade himself have patience; and he composed an ode for the nuptials of his late pupil, which, together with a brief sketch of her ancestral history, he had elegantly printed, according to the Italian usage, and distributed among the family friends; he also made a sonnet to the bridegroom, and these literary tributes were handsomely acknowledged.

He managed a whole year upon the proceeds, and kept a cheerful spirit till the last soldo was spent, inventing one thing after another, and giving much time and money to a new principle of steam propulsion, which, as applied without steam to a small boat on the canal before his door, failed to work, though it had no logical excuse for its delinquency. He tried to get other pupils, but he got none, and he began to dream of going to America. He pinned his faith in all sorts of magnificent possibilities to the names of Franklin, Fulton, and Morse; he was so ignorant of our politics and geography as to suppose us at war with the South American Spaniards, but he knew that English was the language of the North, and he applied himself to the study of it. Heaven only knows what kind of inventor's Utopia, our poor, patent-ridden country appeared to him in these dreams of his, and I can but dimly figure it to myself. But he might very naturally desire to come to a land where the spirit of invention is recognized and fostered, and where he could hope to find that comfort of incentive and companionship which our artists find in Italy.

The idea of the breech-loading cannon had occurred to him suddenly one day, in one of his New-World-ward reveries, and he had made haste to realize it, carefully studying the form and general effect of the Austrian cannon under the gallery of the Ducal Palace, to the high embarrassment of the Croat sentry who paced up and down there, and who did not feel free to order off a priest as he would a civilian. Don Ippolito's model was of admirable finish; he even painted the carriage yellow and black, because that of the original was so, and colored the piece to look like brass; and he lost a day while the paint was drying, after he was otherwise ready to show it to the consul.

He had parted from Ferris with some gleams of comfort, caught chiefly from his kindly manner, but they had died away before nightfall, and this morning he could not rekindle them.

He had had his coffee served to him on the bench, as his frequent custom was, but it stood untasted in the little copper pot beside the dismounted cannon, though it was now ten o'clock, and it was full time he had breakfasted, for he had risen early to perform the matin service for three peasant women, two beggars, a cat, and a paralytic nobleman, in the ancient and beautiful church to which he was attached. He had tried to go about his wonted occupations, but he was still sitting idle before his bench, while his servant gossiped from her balcony to the mistress of the next house, across a calle so deep and narrow that it opened like a mountain chasm beneath them. "It were well if the master read his breviary a little more, instead of always maddening himself with those blessed inventions, that eat more soldi than a Christian, and never come to anything. There he sits before his table, as if he were nailed to his chair, and lets his coffee cool—and God knows I was ready to drink it warm two hours ago—and never looks at me if I open the door twenty times to see whether he has finished. Holy patience! You have not even the advantage of fasting to the glory of God in this house, though you keep Lent the year round. It's the Devil's Lent, *I* say. Eh, Diana! There goes the bell. Who now? Adieu, Lusetta. To meet again, dear. Farewell!"

She ran to another window, and admitted the visitor. It was Ferris, and she went to announce him to her master by the title he had given, while he amused his leisure in the darkness below by falling over a cistern-top, with a loud clattering of his cane on the copper lid, after which he heard the voice of the priest begging him to remain at his convenience a moment till he could descend and show him the way up-stairs. His eyes were not yet used to the obscurity of the narrow entry in which he stood, when he felt a cold hand laid on his, and passively yielded himself to its guidance. He tried to excuse himself for intruding upon Don Ippolito so soon, but the priest in far suppler Italian overwhelmed him with lamentations that he should be so unworthy the honor done him, and ushered his guest into his apartment. He plainly took it for granted that Ferris had come to see his inventions, in compliance with the invitation he had given him the day before, and he made no affectation of delay, though after the excitement of the greetings was past, it was with a quiet dejection that he rose and offered to lead his visitor to his laboratory.

The whole place was an outgrowth of himself; it was his history as well as his character. It recorded his quaint and childish tastes, his restless endeavors, his partial and halting successes. The ante-room in which he had paused with Ferris was painted to look like a grape-arbor, where the vines sprang from the floor, and flourishing up the trellised walls, with many a wanton tendril and flaunting leaf, displayed their lavish clusters of white and purple all over the ceiling. It touched Ferris, when Don Ippolito confessed that this decoration had been the distraction of his own vacant moments, to find that it was like certain grape-arbors he had seen in remote corners of Venice before the doors of degenerate palaces, or forming the entrances of open-air restaurants, and did not seem at all to have been studied from grape-arbors in the country. He perceived the archaic striving for exact truth, and he successfully praised the mechanical skill and love of reality with which it was done; but he was silenced by a collection of paintings in Don Ippolito's parlor, where he had been made to sit down a moment. Hard they were in line, fixed in expression, and opaque in color, these copies of famous masterpieces,—saints of either sex, ascensions, assumptions, martyrdoms, and what not,—and they were not quite comprehensible till Don Ippolito explained that he had made them from such prints of the subjects as he could get, and had colored them after his own fancy. All this, in a city whose art had been the glory of the world for nigh half a thousand years, struck Ferris as yet more comically pathetic than the frescoed grape-arbor; he stared about him for some sort of escape from the pictures, and his eye fell upon a piano and a melodeon placed end to end in a right angle. Don Ippolito, seeing his look of inquiry, sat down and briefly played the same air with a hand upon each instrument.

Ferris smiled. "Don Ippolito, you are another Da Vinci, a universal genius."

"Bagatelles, bagatelles," said the priest pensively; but he rose with greater spirit than he had yet shown, and preceded the consul into the little room that served him for a smithy. It seemed from some peculiarities of shape to have once been an oratory, but it was now begrimed with smoke and dust from the forge which Don Ippolito had set up in it; the embers of a recent fire, the bellows, the pincers, the hammers, and the other implements of the trade, gave it a sinister effect, as if the place of prayer had been invaded by mocking imps, or as if some hapless mortal in contract with the evil powers were here searching, by the help of the adversary, for the forbidden secrets of the metals and of fire. In those days, Ferris was an uncompromising enemy of the theatricalization of Italy, or indeed of anything; but the fancy of the black-robed young priest at work in this place appealed to him all the more potently because of the sort of tragic innocence which seemed to characterize Don Ippolito's expression. He longed intensely to sketch the picture then and there, but he had strength to rebuke the fancy as something that could not make itself intelligible without the help of such accessories as he despised, and he victoriously followed the priest into his larger workshop, where his inventions, complete and incomplete, were stored, and where he had been seated when his visitor arrived. The high windows and the frescoed ceiling were festooned with dusty cobwebs; litter of shavings and whittlings strewed the floor;

mechanical implements and contrivances were everywhere, and Don Ippolito's listlessness seemed to return upon him again at the sight of the familiar disorder. Conspicuous among other objects lay the illogically unsuccessful model of the new principle of steam propulsion, untouched since the day when he had lifted it out of the canal and carried it indoors through the ranks of grinning spectators. From a shelf above it he took down models of a flying-machine and a perpetual motion. "Fantastic researches in the impossible. I never expected results from these experiments, with which I nevertheless once pleased myself," he said, and turned impatiently to various pieces of portable furniture, chairs, tables, bedsteads, which by folding up their legs and tops condensed themselves into flat boxes, developing handles at the side for convenience in carrying. They were painted and varnished, and were in all respects complete; they had indeed won favorable mention at an exposition of the Provincial Society of Arts and Industries, and Ferris could applaud their ingenuity sincerely, though he had his tacit doubts of their usefulness. He fell silent again when Don Ippolito called his notice to a photographic camera, so contrived with straps and springs that you could snatch by its help whatever joy there might be in taking your own photograph; and he did not know what to say of a submarine boat, a four-wheeled water-velocipede, a movable bridge, or the very many other principles and ideas to which Don Ippolito's cunning hand had given shape, more or less imperfect. It seemed to him that they all, however perfect or imperfect, had some fatal defect: they were aspirations toward the impossible, or realizations of the trivial and superfluous. Yet, for all this, they strongly appealed to the painter as the stunted fruit of a talent denied opportunity, instruction, and sympathy. As he looked from them at last to the questioning face of the priest, and considered out of what disheartened and solitary patience they must have come in this city,—dead hundreds of years to all such endeavor,—he could not utter some glib

W. D. Howells

phrases of compliment that he had on his tongue. If Don Ippolito had been taken young, he might perhaps have amounted to something, though this was questionable; but at thirty—as he looked now,—with his undisciplined purposes, and his head full of vagaries of which these things were the tangible witness.... Ferris let his eyes drop again. They fell upon the ruin of the breech-loading cannon, and he said, "Don Ippolito, it's very good of you to take the trouble of showing me these matters, and I hope you'll pardon the ungrateful return, if I cannot offer any definite opinion of them now. They are rather out of my way, I confess. I wish with all my heart I could order an experimental, life-size copy of your breech-loading cannon here, for trial by my government, but I can't; and to tell you the truth, it was not altogether the wish to see these inventions of yours that brought me here to-day."

"Oh," said Don Ippolito, with a mortified air, "I am afraid that I have wearied the Signor Console."

"Not at all, not at all," Ferris made haste to answer, with a frown at his own awkwardness. "But your speaking English yesterday; ... perhaps what I was thinking of is quite foreign to your tastes and possibilities."... He hesitated with a look of perplexity, while Don Ippolito stood before him in an attitude of expectation, pressing the points of his fingers together, and looking curiously into his face. "The case is this," resumed Ferris desperately. "There are two American ladies, friends of mine, sojourning in Venice, who expect to be here till midsummer. They are mother and daughter, and the young lady wants to read and speak Italian with somebody a few hours each day. The question is whether it is quite out of your way or not to give her lessons of this kind. I ask it quite at a venture. I suppose no harm is done, at any rate," and he looked at Don Ippolito with apologetic perturbation.

"No," said the priest, "there is no harm. On the contrary, I am at this moment in a position to consider it a great favor that you do me in offering me this employment. I accept it with the greatest pleasure. Oh!" he cried, breaking by a sudden impulse from the composure with which he had begun to speak, "you don't know what you do for me; you lift me out of despair. Before you came, I had reached one of those passes that seem the last bound of endeavor. But you give me new life. Now I can go on with my experiment. I can at test my gratitude by possessing your native country of the weapon I had designed for it—I am sure of the principle: some slight improvement, perhaps the use of some different explosive, would get over that difficulty you suggested," he said eagerly. "Yes, something can be done. God bless you, my dear little son—I mean—perdoni!—my dear sir."...

"Wait—not so fast," said Ferris with a laugh, yet a little annoyed that a question so purely tentative as his should have met at once such a definite response. "Are you quite sure you can do what they want?" He unfolded to him, as fully as he understood it, Mrs. Vervain's scheme.

Don Ippolito entered into it with perfect intelligence. He said that he had already had charge of the education of a young girl of noble family, and he could therefore the more confidently hope to be useful to this American lady. A light of joyful hope shone in his dreamy eyes, the whole man changed, he assumed the hospitable and caressing host. He conducted Ferris back to his parlor, and making him sit upon the hard sofa that was his hard bed by night, he summoned his servant, and bade her serve them coffee. She closed her lips firmly, and waved her finger before her face, to signify that there was no more coffee. Then he bade her fetch it from the caffe: and he listened with a sort of rapt inattention while Ferris again returned to the subject and explained that he had approached him without first informing the ladies, and that he must regard nothing as final. It was at this point that Don Ippolito, who had understood so clearly what Mrs. Vervain wanted, appeared a little slow to understand; and Ferris had a doubt whether it was from subtlety or from simplicity that the priest seemed not to comprehend the impulse on which he had acted. He finished his coffee in this perplexity, and when he rose to go, Don Ippolito followed him down to the street-door, and preserved him from a second encounter with the cistern-top.

"But, Don Ippolito—remember! I make no engagement for the ladies, whom you must see before anything is settled," said Ferris.

"Surely,—surely!" answered the priest, and he remained smiling at the door till the American turned the next corner. Then he went back to his work-room, and took up the broken model from the bench. But he could not work at it now, he could not work at anything; he began to walk up and down the floor.

"Could he really have been so stupid because his mind was on his ridiculous cannon?" wondered Ferris as he sauntered frowning away; and he tried to prepare his own mind for his meeting with the Vervains, to whom he must now go at once. He felt abused and victimized. Yet it was an amusing experience, and he found himself able to interest both of the ladies in it. The younger had received him as coldly as the forms of greeting would allow; but as he talked she drew nearer him with a reluctant haughtiness which he noted. He turned the more conspicuously towards Mrs. Vervain. "Well, to make a long story short," he said, "I couldn't discourage Don Ippolito. He refused to be dismayed—as I should have been at the notion of teaching Miss Vervain. I didn't arrange with him not to fall in love with her as his secular predecessors have done—it seemed superfluous. But you can mention it to him if you like. In fact," said Ferris, suddenly addressing the daughter, "you might make the stipulation yourself, Miss Vervain."

She looked at him a moment with a sort of defenseless pain that made him ashamed; and then walked away from him towards the window, with a frank resentment that made him smile, as he continued, "But I suppose you would like to have some explanation of my motive in precipitating Don Ippolito upon you in this way, when I told you only yesterday that he wouldn't do at all; in fact I think myself that I've behaved rather fickle-mindedly—for a representative of the country. But I'll tell you; and you won't be surprised to learn that I acted from mixed motives. I'm not at all sure that he'll do; I've had awful misgivings about it since I left him, and I'm glad of the chance to make a clean breast of it. When I came to think the matter over last night, the fact that he had taught himself English—with the help of an Irishman for the pronunciation—seemed to promise that he'd have the right sort of sympathy with your scheme, and it showed that he must have something practical about him, too. And here's where the selfish admixture comes in. I didn't have your interests solely in mind when I went to see Don Ippolito. I hadn't been able to get rid of him; he stuck in my thought. I fancied he might be glad of the pay of a teacher, and—I had half a notion to ask him to let me paint him. It was an even chance whether I should try to secure him for Miss Vervain, or for Art—as they call it. Miss Vervain won because she could pay him, and I didn't see how Art could. I can bring him round any time; and that's the whole inconsequent business. My consolation is that I've left you perfectly free. There's nothing decided."

"Thanks," said Mrs. Vervain; "then it's all settled. You can bring him as soon as you like, to our new place. We've taken that apartment we looked at the other day, and we're going into it this afternoon. Here's the landlord's letter," she added, drawing a paper out of her pocket. "If he's cheated us, I suppose you can see justice done. I didn't want to trouble you before."

"You're a woman of business, Mrs. Vervain," said Ferris. "The man's a perfect Jew—or a perfect Christian, one ought to say in Venice; we true believers do gouge so much, more infamously here—and you let him get you in black and white before you come to me. Well," he continued, as he glanced at the paper, "you've done it! He makes you pay one half too much. However, it's cheap enough; twice as cheap as your hotel."

"But I don't care for cheapness. I hate to be imposed upon. What's to be done about it?"

"Nothing; if he has your letter as you have his. It's a bargain, and you must stand to it."

"A bargain? Oh nonsense, now, Mr. Ferris. This is merely a note of mutual understanding."

"Yes, that's one way of looking at it. The Civil Tribunal would call it a binding agreement of the closest tenure,—if you want to go to law about it."

"I *will* go to law about it."

"Oh no, you won't—unless you mean to spend your remaining days and all your substance in Venice. Come, you haven't done so badly, Mrs. Vervain. I don't call four rooms, completely furnished for housekeeping, with that lovely garden, at all dear at eleven francs a day. Besides, the landlord is a man of excellent feeling, sympathetic and obliging, and a perfect gentleman, though he is such an outrageous scoundrel. He'll cheat you, of course, in whatever he can; you must look out for that; but he'll do you any sort of little neighborly kindness. Good-by," said Ferris, getting to the door before Mrs. Vervain could intercept him. "I'll come to your new place this evening to see how you are pleased."

"Florida," said Mrs. Vervain, "this is outrageous."

"I wouldn't mind it, mother. We pay very little, after all."

"Yes, but we pay too much. That's what I can't bear. And as you said yesterday, I don't think Mr. Ferris's manners are quite respectful to me."

"He only told you the truth; I think he advised you for the best. The matter couldn't be helped now."

"But I call it a want of feeling to speak the truth so bluntly."

"We won't have to complain of that in our landlord, it seems," said Florida. "Perhaps not in our priest, either," she added.

"Yes, that *was* kind of Mr. Ferris," said Mrs. Vervain. "It was thoroughly thoughtful and considerate—what I call an instance of true delicacy. I'm really quite curious to see him. Don Ippolito! How very odd to call a priest *Don*! I should have said Padre. Don always makes you think of a Spanish cavalier. Don Rodrigo: something like that."

They went on to talk, desultorily, of Don Ippolito, and what he might be like. In speaking of him the day before, Ferris had hinted at some mysterious sadness in him; and to hint of sadness in a man always interests women in him, whether they are old or young: the old have suffered, the young

W. D. Howells

forebode suffering. Their interest in Don Ippolito had not been diminished by what Ferris had told them of his visit to the priest's house and of the things he had seen there; for there had always been the same strain of pity in his laughing account, and he had imparted none of his doubts to them. They did not talk as if it were strange that Ferris should do to-day what he had yesterday said he would not do; perhaps as women they could not find such a thing strange; but it vexed him more and more as he went about all afternoon thinking of his inconsistency, and wondering whether he had not acted rashly.

IV

The palace in which Mrs. Vervain had taken an apartment
fronted on a broad campo, and hung its empty marble
balconies from gothic windows above a silence scarcely to
be matched elsewhere in Venice. The local pharmacy, the
caffe, the grocery, the fruiterer's, the other shops with which
every Venetian campo is furnished, had each a certain life
about it, but it was a silent life, and at midday a frowsy-
headed woman clacking across the flags in her wooden-
heeled shoes made echoes whose garrulity was interrupted
by no other sound. In the early morning, when the lid of the
public cistern in the centre of the campo was unlocked, there
was a clamor of voices and a clangor of copper vessels, as
the housewives of the neighborhood and the local force of
strong-backed Frinlan water-girls drew their day's supply of
water; and on that sort of special parochial holiday, called a
sagra, the campo hummed and clattered and shrieked with a
multitude celebrating the day around the stands where
pumpkin seeds and roast pumpkin and anisette-water were
sold, and before the movable kitchen where cakes were fried
in caldrons of oil, and uproariously offered to the crowd by
the cook, who did not suffer himself to be embarrassed by
the rival drama of adjoining puppet-shows, but continued to
bellow forth his bargains all day long and far into the night,
when the flames under his kettles painted his visage a fine
crimson. The sagra once over, however, the campo relapsed

W. D. Howells

into its habitual silence, and no one looking at the front of the palace would have thought of it as a place for distraction-seeking foreign sojourners. But it was not on this side that the landlord tempted his tenants; his principal notice of lodgings to let was affixed to the water-gate of the palace, which opened on a smaller channel so near the Grand Canal that no wandering eye could fail to see it. The portal was a tall arch of Venetian gothic tipped with a carven flame; steps of white Istrian stone descended to the level of the lowest ebb, irregularly embossed with barnacles, and dabbling long fringes of soft green sea-mosses in the rising and falling tide. Swarms of water-bugs and beetles played over the edges of the steps, and crabs scuttled side-wise into deeper water at the approach of a gondola. A length of stone-capped brick wall, to which patches of stucco still clung, stretched from the gate on either hand under cover of an ivy that flung its mesh of shining green from within, where there lurked a lovely garden, stately, spacious for Venice, and full of a delicious, half-sad surprise for whoso opened upon it. In the midst it had a broken fountain, with a marble naiad standing on a shell, and looking saucier than the sculptor meant, from having lost the point of her nose, nymphs and fauns, and shepherds and shepherdesses, her kinsfolk, coquetted in and out among the greenery in flirtation not to be embarrassed by the fracture of an arm, or the casting of a leg or so; one lady had no head, but she was the boldest of all. In this garden there were some mulberry and pomegranate trees, several of which hung about the fountain with seats in their shade, and for the rest there seemed to be mostly roses and oleanders, with other shrubs of a kind that made the greatest show of blossom and cost the least for tendance. A wide terrace stretched across the rear of the palace, dropping to the garden path by a flight of balustraded steps, and upon this terrace opened the long windows of Mrs. Vervain's parlor and dining-room. Her landlord owned only the first story and the basement of the palace, in some corner of which he cowered with his servants, his taste for pictures and *bric-a-brac*, and his little branch of inquiry into Venetian history, whatever it was, ready to let himself or anything he had for hire at a moment's notice, but very pleasant, gentle, and unobtrusive; a cheat and a liar, but of a kind heart and sympathetic manners. Under his protection Mrs. Vervain set up her impermanent household gods. The apartment was taken only from week to week, and as she freely explained to the *padrone* hovering about with offers of service, she knew herself too well ever to unpack anything that would not spoil by remaining packed. She made her trunks yield all the appliances necessary for an invalid's comfort, and then left them in a state to be strapped and transported to the station within half a day after the desire of change or the exigencies of her feeble health caused her going. Everything for housekeeping was furnished with the rooms. There was a gondolier and a sort of house-servant in the employ of the landlord, of whom Mrs. Vervain hired them, and she caressingly dismissed the padrone at an early moment after her arrival, with the charge to find a maid for herself and daughter. As if she had been waiting at the next door this maid appeared promptly, and being Venetian, and in domestic service, her name was of course Nina. Mrs. Vervain now said to Florida that everything was perfect, and contentedly began her life in Venice by telling Mr. Ferris, when he came in the evening, that he could bring Don Ippolito the day after the morrow, if he liked.

She and Florida sat on the terrace waiting for them on the morning named, when Ferris, with the priest in his clerical best, came up the garden path in the sunny light. Don Ippolito's best was a little poverty-stricken; he had faltered a while, before leaving home, over the sad choice between a shabby cylinder hat of obsolete fashion and his well-worn three-cornered priestly beaver, and had at last put on the latter with a sigh. He had made his servant polish the buckles of his shoes, and instead of a band of linen round his throat, he wore a strip ot cloth covered with small white beads, edged above and below with a single row of pale blue ones.

As he mounted the steps with Ferris, Mrs. Vervain came forward a little to meet them, while Florida rose and stood beside her chair in a sort of proud suspense and timidity. The elder lady was in that black from which she had so seldom been able to escape; but the daughter wore a dress of delicate green, in which she seemed a part of the young season that everywhere clothed itself in the same tint. The sunlight fell upon her blonde hair, melting into its light gold; her level brows frowned somewhat with the glance of scrutiny which she gave the dark young priest, who was making his stately bow to her mother, and trying to answer her English greetings in the same tongue.

"My daughter," said Mrs. Vervain, and Don Ippolito made another low bow, and then looked at the girl with a sort of frank and melancholy wonder, as she turned and exchanged a few words with Ferris, who was assailing her seriousness and hauteur with unabashed levity of compliment. A quick light flashed and fled in her cheek as she talked, and the fringes of her serious, asking eyes swept slowly up and down as she bent them upon him a moment before she broke abruptly, not coquettishly, away from him, and moved towards her mother, while Ferris walked off to the other end of the terrace, with a laugh. Mrs. Vervain and the priest were trying each other in French, and not making great advance; he explained to Florida in Italian, and she answered him hesitatingly; whereupon he praised her Italian in set phrase.

"Thank you," said the girl sincerely, "I have tried to learn. I hope," she added as before, "you can make me see how little I know." The deprecating wave of the hand with which Don Ippolito appealed to her from herself, seemed arrested midway by his perception of some novel quality in her. He said gravely that he should try to be of use, and then the two stood silent.

"Come, Mr. Ferris," called out Mrs. Vervain, "breakfast is ready, and I want you to take me in."

"Too much honor," said the painter, coming forward and offering his arm, and Mrs. Vervain led the way indoors.

"I suppose I ought to have taken Don Ippolito's arm," she confided in under-tone, "but the fact is, our French is so unlike that we don't understand each other very well."

"Oh," returned Ferris, "I've known Italians and Americans whom Frenchmen themselves couldn't understand."

"You see it's an American breakfast," said Mrs. Vervain with a critical glance at the table before she sat down. "All but hot bread; *that* you *can't* have," and Don Ippolito was for the first time in his life confronted by a breakfast of hot beef-steak, eggs and toast, fried potatoes, and coffee with milk, with a choice of tea. He subdued all signs of the wonder he must have felt, and beyond cutting his meat into little bits before eating it, did nothing to betray his strangeness to the feast.

The breakfast had passed off very pleasantly, with occasional lapses. "We break down under the burden of so many languages," said Ferris. "It is an *embarras de richesses*. Let us fix upon a common maccheronic. May I trouble you for a poco piu di sugar dans mon cafe, Mrs. Vervain? What do you think of the bellazza de ce weather magnifique, Don Ippolito?"

"How ridiculous!" said Mrs. Vervain in a tone of fond

admiration aside to Don Ippolito, who smiled, but shrank from contributing to the new tongue.

"Very well, then," said the painter. "I shall stick to my native Bergamask for the future; and Don Ippolito may translate for the foreign ladies."

He ended by speaking English with everybody; Don Ippolito eked out his speeches to Mrs. Vervain in that tongue with a little French; Florida, conscious of Ferris's ironical observance, used an embarrassed but defiant Italian with the priest.

"I'm so pleased!" said Mrs. Vervain, rising when Ferris said that he must go, and Florida shook hands with both guests.

"Thank you, Mrs. Vervain; I could have gone before, if I'd thought you would have liked it," answered the painter.

"Oh nonsense, now," returned the lady. "You know what I mean. I'm perfectly delighted with him," she continued, getting Ferris to one side, "and I *know* he must have a good accent. So very kind of you. Will you arrange with him about the pay?—such a *shame*! Thanks. Then I needn't say anything to him about that. I'm so glad I had him to breakfast the first day; though Florida thought not. Of course, one needn't keep it up. But seriously, it isn't an ordinary case, you know."

Ferris laughed at her with a sort of affectionate disrespect, and said good-by. Don Ippolito lingered for a while to talk over the proposed lessons, and then went, after more elaborate adieux. Mrs. Vervain remained thoughtful a moment before she said:—

"That was rather droll, Florida."

"What, mother?"

"His cutting his meat into small bites, before he began to eat. But perhaps it's the Venetian custom. At any rate, my dear, he's a gentleman in virtue of his profession, and I couldn't do less than ask him to breakfast. He has beautiful manners; and if he must take snuff, I suppose it's neater to carry two handkerchiefs, though it does look odd. I wish he wouldn't take snuff."

"I don't see why we need care, mother. At any fate, we cannot help it."

"That's true, my dear. And his nails. Now when they're spread out on a book, you know, to keep it open,—won't it be unpleasant?"

"They seem to have just such fingernails all over Europe—except in England."

"Oh, yes; I know it. I dare say we shouldn't care for it in him, if he didn't seem so very nice otherwise. How handsome he is!"

V

It was understood that Don Ippolito should come every morning at ten o'clock, and read and talk with Miss Vervain for an hour or two; but Mrs. Vervain's hospitality was too aggressive for the letter of the agreement. She oftener had him to breakfast at nine, for, as she explained to Ferris, she could not endure to have him feel that it was a mere mercenary transaction, and there was no limit fixed for the lessons on these days. When she could, she had Ferris come, too, and she missed him when he did not come. "I like that bluntness of his," she professed to her daughter, "and I don't mind his making light of me. You are so apt to be heavy if you're not made light of occasionally. I certainly shouldn't want a *son* to be so respectful and obedient as you are, my dear."

The painter honestly returned her fondness, and with not much greater reason. He saw that she took pleasure in his talk, and enjoyed it even when she did not understand it; and this is a kind of flattery not easy to resist. Besides, there was very little ladies' society in Venice in those times, and Ferris, after trying the little he could get at, had gladly denied himself its pleasures, and consorted with the young men he met at the caffe's, or in the Piazza. But when the Vervains came, they recalled to him the younger days in which he had delighted in the companionship of women. After so long disuse, it was charming to be with a beautiful girl who neither regarded him with distrust nor expected him to ask her in marriage because he sat alone with her, rode out with her in a gondola, walked with her, read with her. All young men like a house in which no ado is made about their coming and going, and Mrs. Vervain perfectly understood the art of letting him make himself at home. He perceived with amusement that this amiable lady, who never did an ungraceful thing nor wittingly said an ungracious one, was very much of a Bohemian at heart,—the gentlest and most blameless of the tribe, but still lawless,—whether from her campaigning married life, or the rovings of her widowhood, or by natural disposition; and that Miss Vervain was inclined to be conventionally strict, but with her irregular training was at a loss for rules by which to check her mother's little waywardnesses. Her anxious perplexity, at times, together with her heroic obedience and unswerving loyalty to her mother had something pathetic as well as amusing in it. He saw her tried almost to tears by her mother's helpless frankness,—for Mrs. Vervain was apparently one of those ladies whom the intolerable surprise of having anything come into their heads causes instantly to say or do it,—and he observed that she never tried to pass off her endurance with any feminine arts; but seemed to defy him to think what he would of it. Perhaps she was not able to do otherwise: he thought of her at times as a person wholly abandoned to the truth. Her pride was on the alert against him; she may have imagined that he was covertly smiling at her, and she no doubt tasted the ironical flavor of much of his talk and behavior, for in those days he liked to qualify his devotion to the Vervains with a certain nonchalant slight, which, while the mother openly enjoyed it, filled the daughter with anger and apprehension. Quite at random, she visited points of his informal manner with unmeasured reprisal; others, for which he might have blamed himself, she passed over with strange caprice. Sometimes this attitude of hers provoked him, and sometimes it disarmed him; but whether they were at feud, or keeping an armed truce, or, as now and then happened, were in an *entente cordiale* which he found very charming, the thing that he always contrived to treat with silent respect and forbearance in Miss Vervain was that sort of aggressive tenderness with which she hastened to shield the foibles of her mother. That was something very good in her pride, he finally decided. At the same time, he did not pretend to understand the curious filial self-sacrifice which it involved.

Another thing in her that puzzled him was her devoutness. Mrs. Vervain could with difficulty be got to church, but her daughter missed no service of the English ritual in the old palace where the British and American tourists assembled once a week with their guide-books in one pocket and their prayer-books in the other, and buried the tomahawk under the altar. Mr. Ferris was often sent with her; and then his thoughts, which were a young man's, wandered from the service to the beautiful girl at his side,—the golden head that punctiliously bowed itself at the proper places in the liturgy: the full lips that murmured the responses; the silken lashes that swept her pale cheeks as she perused the morning lesson. He knew that the Vervains were not Episcopalians when at home, for Mrs. Vervain had told him so, and that Florida went to the English service because there was no other. He conjectured that perhaps her touch of ritualism came from mere love of any form she could make sure of.

The servants in Mrs. Vervain's lightly ordered household, with the sympathetic quickness of the Italians, learned to use him as the next friend of the family, and though they may have had their decorous surprise at his untrammeled footing, they probably excused the whole relation as a phase of that foreign eccentricity to which their nation is so amiable. If they were not able to cast the same mantle of charity over Don Ippolito's allegiance,—and doubtless they had their reserves concerning such frankly familiar treatment of so dubious a character as priest,—still as a priest they stood somewhat in awe of him; they had the spontaneous loyalty of their race to the people they served, and they never intimated by a look that they found it strange when Don Ippolito freely came and went. Mrs. Vervain had quite adopted him into her family; while her daughter seemed more at ease with him than with Ferris, and treated him with a grave politeness which had something also of compassion and of child-like reverence in it. Ferris observed that she was always particularly careful of his supposable sensibilities as a Roman Catholic, and that the priest was oddly indifferent to this deference, as if it would have mattered very little to him whether his church was spared or not. He had a way of lightly avoiding, Ferris fancied, not only religious points on which they could disagree, but all phases of religion as matters of indifference. At such times Miss Vervain relaxed her reverential attitude, and used him with something like rebuke, as if it did not please her to have the representative of even an alien religion slight his office; as if her respect were for his priesthood and her compassion for him personally. That was rather hard for Don Ippolito, Ferris thought, and waited to see him snubbed outright some day, when he should behave without sufficient gravity.

The blossoms came and went upon the pomegranate and almond trees in the garden, and some of the earliest roses were in their prime; everywhere was so full leaf that the wantonest of the strutting nymphs was forced into a sort of decent seclusion, but the careless naiad of the fountain burnt in sunlight that subtly increased its fervors day by day, and it was no longer beginning to be warm, it was warm, when one morning Ferris and Miss Vervain sat on the steps of the terrace, waiting for Don Ippolito to join them at breakfast.

By this time the painter was well on with the picture of Don

W. D. Howells

Ippolito which the first sight of the priest had given him a longing to paint, and he had been just now talking of it with Miss Vervain.

"But why do you paint him simply as a priest?" she asked. "I should think you would want to make him the centre of some famous or romantic scene," she added, gravely looking into his eyes as he sat with his head thrown back against the balustrade.

"No, I doubt if you *think*," answered Ferris, "or you'd see that a Venetian priest doesn't need any tawdry accessories. What do you want? Somebody administering the extreme unction to a victim of the Council of Ten? A priest stepping into a confessional at the Frari— tomb of Canova in the distance, perspective of one of the naves, and so forth—with his eye on a pretty devotee coming up to unburden her conscience? I've no patience with the follies people, think and say about Venice!"

Florida stared in haughty question at the painter.

"You're no worse than the rest," he continued with indifference to her anger at his bluntness. "You all think that there can be no picture of Venice without a gondola or a Bridge of Sighs in it. Have you ever read the Merchant of Venice, or Othello? There isn't a boat nor a bridge nor a canal mentioned in either of them; and yet they breathe and pulsate with the very life of Venice. I'm going to try to paint a Venetian priest so that you'll know him without a bit of conventional Venice near him."

"It was Shakespeare who wrote those plays," said Florida. Ferris bowed in mock suffering from her sarcasm. "You'd better have some sort of symbol in your picture of a Venetian priest, or people will wonder why you came so far to paint

Father O'Brien."

"I don't say I shall succeed," Ferris answered. "In fact I've made one failure already, and I'm pretty well on with a second; but the principle is right, all the same. I don't expect everybody to see the difference between Don Ippolito and Father O'Brien. At any rate, what I'm going to paint *at* is the lingering pagan in the man, the renunciation first of the inherited nature, and then of a personality that would have enjoyed the world. I want to show that baffled aspiration, apathetic despair, and rebellious longing which you caten in his face When he's off his guard, and that suppressed look which is the characteristic expression of all Austrian Venice. Then," said Ferris laughing, "T must work in that small suspicion of Jesuit which there is in every priest. But it's quite possible I may make a Father O'Brien of him."

"You won't make a Don Ippolito of him," said Florida, after serious consideration of his face to see whether he was quite in earnest, "if you put all that into him. He has the simplest and openest look in the world," she added warmly, "and there's neither pagan, nor martyr, nor rebel in it."

Ferris laughed again. "Excuse me; I don't think you know. I can convince you."...

Florida rose, and looking down the garden path said, "He's coming;" and as Don Ippolito drew near, his face lighting up with a joyous and innocent smile, she continued absently, "he's got on new stockings, and a different coat and hat."

The stockings were indeed new and the hat was not the accustomed *nicchio*, but a new silk cylinder with a very worldly, curling brim. Don Ippolito's coat, also, was of a more mundane cut than the talare; he wore a waistcoat and small-clothes, meeting the stockings at the knee with a sprightly buckle. His person showed no traces of the snuff with which it used to be so plentifully dusted; in fact, he no longer took snuff in the presence of the ladies. The first week he had noted an inexplicable uneasiness in them when he drew forth that blue cotton handkerchief after the solace of a pinch shortly afterwards, being alone with Florida, he saw her give a nervous start at its appearance. He blushed violently, and put it back into the pocket from which he had half drawn it, and whence it never emerged again in her presence. The contessina his former pupil had not shown any aversion to Don Ippolito's snuff or his blue handkerchief; but then the contessina had never rebuked his finger-nails by the tints of rose and ivory with which Miss Vervain's hands bewildered him. It was a little droll how anxiously he studied the ways of these Americans, and conformed to them as far as he knew. His English grew rapidly in their society, and it happened sometimes that the only Italian in the day's lesson was what he read with Florida, for she always yielded to her mother's wish to talk, and Mrs. Vervain preferred the ease of her native tongue. He was Americanizing in that good lady's hands as fast as she could transform him, and he listened to her with trustful reverence, as to a woman of striking though eccentric mind. Yet he seemed finally to refer every point to Florida, as if with an intuition of steadier and stronger character in her; and now, as he ascended the terrace steps in his modified costume, he looked intently at her. She swept him from head to foot with a glance, and then gravely welcomed him with unchanged countenance.

At the same moment Mrs. Vervain came out through one of the long windows, and adjusting her glasses, said with a start, "Why, my dear Don Ippolito, I shouldn't have known you!"

"Indeed, madama?" asked the priest—with a painful smile. "Is it so great a change? We can wear this dress as well as the other, if we please."

"Why, of course it's very becoming and all that; but it does look so out of character," Mrs. Vervain said, leading the way to the breakfast-room. "It's like seeing a military man in a civil coat."

"It must be a great relief to lay aside the uniform now and then, mother," said Florida, as they sat down. "I can remember that papa used to be glad to get out of his."

"Perfectly wild," assented Mrs. Vervain. "But he never seemed the same person. Soldiers and—clergymen—are so much more stylish in their own dress—not stylish, exactly, but taking; don't you know?"

"There, Don Ippolito," interposed Ferris, "you had better put on your talare and your nicchio again. Your *abbate's* dress isn't acceptable, you see."

The painter spoke in Italian, but Don Ippolito answered— with certain blunders which it would be tedious to repro- duce—in his patient, conscientious English, half sadly, half playfully, and glancing at Florida, before he turned to Mrs. Vervain, "You are as rigid as the rest of the world, madama. I thought you would like this dress, but it seems that you think it a masquerade. As madamigella says, it is a relief to lay aside the uniform, now and then, for us who fight the spiritual enemies as well as for the other soldiers. There was one time, when I was younger and in the subdiaconate orders, that I put off the priest's dress altogether, and wore citizen's clothes, not an abbate's suit like this. We were in Padua, another young priest and I, my nearest and only friend, and for a whole night we walked about the streets in that dress, meeting the students, as they strolled singing through the moonlight; we went to the theatre and to the caffe,—we smoked cigars, all the time laughing and trembling to think of the tonsure under our hats. But in the morning we had to put on the stockings and the talare and the nicchio again."

Don Ippolito gave a melancholy laugh. He had thrust the corner of his napkin into his collar; seeing that Ferris had not his so, he twitched it out, and made a feint of its having been all the time in his lap. Every one was silent as if something shocking had been said; Florida looked with grave rebuke at Don Ippolito, whose story affected Ferris like that of some girl's adventure in men's clothes. He was in terror lest Mrs. Vervain should be going to say it was like that; she was going to say something; he made haste to forestall her, and turn the talk on other things.

The next day the priest came in his usual dress, and he did not again try to escape from it.

VI

One afternoon, as Don Ippolito was posing to Perris for his picture of A Venetian Priest, the painter asked, to make talk, "Have you hit upon that new explosive yet, which is to utilize your breech-loading cannon? Or are you engaged upon something altogether new?"

"No," answered the other uneasily, "I have not touched the cannon since that day you saw it at my house; and as for other things, I have not been able to put my mind to them. I have made a few trifles which I have ventured to offer the ladies."

Ferris had noticed the ingenious reading-desk which Don Ippolito had presented to Florida, and the footstool, contrived with springs and hinges so that it would fold up into the compass of an ordinary portfolio, which Mrs. Vervain carried about with her.

An odd look, which the painter caught at and missed, came into the priest's face, as he resumed: "I suppose it is the distraction of my new occupation, and of the new acquaintances—so very strange to me in every way—that I have made in your amiable country-women, which hinders me from going about anything in earnest, now that their munificence has enabled me to pursue my aims with greater advantages than ever before. But this idle mood will pass, and in the mean time I am very happy. They are real angels, and madama is a true original."

"Mrs. Vervain is rather peculiar," said the painter, retiring a few paces from his picture, and quizzing it through his half-closed eyes. "She is a woman who has had affliction enough to turn a stronger head than hers could ever have been," he added kindly. "But she has the best heart in the world. In fact," he burst forth, "she is the most extraordinary combination of perfect fool and perfect lady I ever saw."

"Excuse me; I don't understand," blankly faltered Don Ippolito.

"No; and I'm afraid I couldn't explain to you," answered Ferris.

There was a silence for a time, broken at last by Don Ippolito, who asked, "Why do you not marry madamigella?"

He seemed not to feel that there was anything out of the way in the question, and Ferris was too well used to the childlike directness of the most maneuvering of races to be surprised. Yet he was displeased, as he would not have been if Don Ippolito were not a priest. He was not of the type of priests whom the American knew from the prejudice and distrust of the Italians; he was alienated from his clerical fellows by all the objects of his life, and by a reciprocal dislike. About other priests there were various scandals; but Don Ippolito was like that pretty match-girl of the Piazza of whom it was Venetianly answered, when one asked if so sweet a face were not innocent, "Oh yes, she is mad!" He was of a purity so blameless that he was reputed crack-brained by the caffe-gossip that in Venice turns its searching light upon whomever you mention; and from his own association with the man Ferris perceived in him an apparent single-heartedness such as no man can have but the rarest of Italians. He was the albino of his species; a gray crow, a white fly; he was really this, or he knew how to seem it with an art far beyond any common deceit. It was the half expectation of coming sometime upon the lurking duplicity in Don Ippolito, that continually enfeebled the painter in his attempts to portray his Venetian priest, and that gave its undecided, unsatisfactory character to the picture before him—its weak hardness, its provoking superficiality. He expressed the traits of melancholy and loss that he imagined in him, yet he always was tempted to leave the picture with a touch of something sinister in it, some airy and subtle shadow of selfish design.

He stared hard at Don Ippolito while this perplexity filled his mind, for the hundredth time; then he said stiffly, "I don't know. I don't want to marry anybody. Besides," he added, relaxing into a smile of helpless amusement, "it's possible that Miss Vervain might not want to marry me."

"As to that," replied Don Ippolito, "you never can tell. All young girls desire to be married, I suppose," he continued with a sigh. "She is very beautiful, is she not? It is seldom that we see such a blonde in Italy. Our blondes are dark; they have auburn hair and blue eyes, but their complexions are thick. Miss Vervain is blonde as the morning light; the sun's gold is in her hair, his noonday whiteness in her dazzling throat; the flush of his coming is on her lips; she might utter the dawn!"

"You're a poet, Don Ippolito," laughed the painter. "What property of the sun is in her angry-looking eyes?"

"His fire! Ah, that is her greatest charm! Those strange eyes of hers, they seem full of tragedies. She looks made to be the heroine of some stormy romance; and yet how simply patient and good she is!"

"Yes," said Ferris, who often responded in English to the priest's Italian; and he added half musingly in his own tongue, after a moment, "but I don't think it would be safe to count upon her. I'm afraid she has a bad temper. At any rate, I always expect to see smoke somewhere when I look at those eyes of hers. She has wonderful self-control, however; and I don't exactly understand why. Perhaps people of strong impulses have strong wills to overrule them; it seems no more than fair."

"Is it the custom," asked Don Ippolito, after a moment, "for the American young ladies always to address their mammas as *mother?*"

"No; that seems to be a peculiarity of Miss Vervain's. It's a little formality that I should say served to hold Mrs. Vervain in check."

"Do you mean that it repulses her?"

"Not at all. I don't think I could explain," said Ferris with a certain air of regretting to have gone so far in comment on the Vervains. He added recklessly, "Don't you see that Mrs. Vervain sometimes does and says things that embarrass her daughter, and that Miss Vervain seems to try to restrain her?"

"I thought," returned Don Ippolito meditatively, "that the signorina was always very tenderly submissive to her mother."

"Yes, so she is," said the painter dryly, and looked in annoyance from the priest to the picture, and from the picture to the priest.

After a minute Don Ippolito said, "They must be very rich to live as they do."

"I don't know about that," replied Ferris. "Americans spend and save in ways different from the Italians. I dare say the Vervains find Venice very cheap after London and Paris and Berlin."

"Perhaps," said Don Ippolito, "if they were rich you would be in a position to marry her."

"I should not marry Miss Vervain for her money," answered the painter, sharply.

"No, but if you loved her, the money would enable you to marry her."

"Listen to me, Don Ippolito. I never said that I loved Miss Vervain, and I don't know how you feel warranted in speaking to me about the matter. Why do you do so?"

"I? Why? I could not but imagine that you must love her. Is there anything wrong in speaking of such things? Is it contrary to the American custom? I ask pardon from my heart if I have done anything amiss."

"There is no offense,' said the painter, with a laugh," and I don't wonder you thought I ought to be in love with Miss Vervain. She *is* beautiful, and I believe she's good. But if men had to marry because women were beautiful and good, there isn't one of us could live single a day. Besides, I'm the victim of another passion,—I'm laboring under an unrequited affection for Art."

"Then you do *not* love her?" asked Don Ippolito, eagerly.

"So far as I'm advised at present, no, I don't."

"It is strange!" said the priest, absently, but with a glowing face.

He quitted the painter's and walked swiftly homeward with a triumphant buoyancy of step. A subtle content diffused itself over his face, and a joyful light burnt in his deep eyes. He sat down before the piano and organ as he had arranged them, and began to strike their keys in unison; this seemed to him for the first time childish. Then he played some lively bars on the piano alone; they sounded too light and trivial, and he turned to the other instrument. As the plaint of the reeds arose, it filled his sense like a solemn organ-music, and transfigured the place; the notes swelled to the ample vault of a church, and at the high altar he was celebrating the mass in his sacerdotal robes. He suddenly caught his fingers away from the keys; his breast heaved, he hid his face in his hands.

VII

Ferris stood cleaning his palette, after Don Ippolito was gone, scraping the colors together with his knife and neatly buttering them on the palette's edge, while he wondered what the priest meant by pumping him in that way. Nothing, he supposed, and yet it was odd. Of course she had a bad temper....

He put on his hat and coat and strolled vaguely forth, and in an hour or two came by a roundabout course to the gondola station nearest his own house. There he stopped, and after an absent contemplation of the boats, from which the gondoliers were clamoring for his custom, he stepped into one and ordered the man to row him to a gate on a small canal opposite. The gate opened, at his ringing, into the garden of the Vervains.

Florida was sitting alone on a bench near the fountain. It was no longer a ruined fountain; the broken-nosed naiad held a pipe above her head, and from this rose a willowy spray high enough to catch some colors of the sunset then striking into the garden, and fell again in a mist around her, making her almost modest.

"What does this mean?" asked Ferris, carelessly taking the young girl's hand. "I thought this lady's occupation was gone."

"Don Ippolito repaired the fountain for the landlord, and he agreed to pay for filling the tank that feeds it," said Florida. "He seems to think it a hard bargain, for he only lets it play about half an hour a day. But he says it's very ingeniously mended. He didn't believe it could be done. It *is* pretty.

"It is, indeed," said the painter, with a singular desire, going through him like a pang, likewise to do something for Miss Vervain. "Did you go to Don Ippolito's house the other day, to see his traps?"

"Yes; we were very much interested. I was sorry that I knew so little about inventions. Do you think there are many practical ideas amongst his things? I hope there are—he seemed so proud and pleased to show them. Shouldn't you think he had some real inventive talent?"

"Yes, I think he has; but I know as little about the matter as you do." He sat down beside her, and picking up a twig from the gravel, pulled the bark off in silence. Then, "Miss Vervain," he said, knitting his brows, as he always did when he had something on his conscience and meant to ease it at any cost, "I'm the dog that fetches a bone and carries a bone; I talked Don Ippolito over with you, the other day, and now I've been talking you over with him. But I've the grace to say that I'm ashamed of myself."

"Why need you be ashamed?" asked Florida. "You said no harm of him. Did you of us?"

"Not exactly; but I don't think it was quite my business to discuss you at all. I think you can't let people alone too much. For my part, if I try to characterize my friends, I fail to do them perfect justice, of course; and yet the imperfect result remains representative of them in my mind; it limits them and fixes them; and I can't get them back again into the undefined and the ideal where they really belong. One ought never to speak of the faults of one's friends: it mutilates them; they can never be the same afterwards."

"So you have been talking of my faults," said Florida, breathing quickly. "Perhaps you could tell me of them to my face."

"I should have to say that unfairness was one of them. But that is common to the whole sex. I never said I was talking of your faults. I declared against doing so, and you immediately infer that my motive is remorse. I don't know that you have any faults. They may be virtues in disguise. There is a charm even in unfairness. Well, I did Bay that I thought you had a quick temper,"—

Florida colored violently.

—"but now I see that I was mistaken," said Ferris with a laugh.

"May I ask what else you said?" demanded the young girl haughtily.

"Oh, that would be a betrayal of confidence," said Ferris, unaffected by her hauteur.

"Then why have you mentioned the matter to me at all?"

"I wanted to clear my conscience, I suppose, and sin again. I wanted to talk with you about Don Ippolito."

Florida looked with perplexity at Ferris's face, while her own slowly cooled and paled.

"What did you want to say of him?" she asked calmly.

"I hardly know how to put it: that he puzzles me, to begin with. You know I feel somewhat responsible for him."

"Yes."

"Of course, I never should have thought of him, if it hadn't been for your mother's talk that morning coming back from San Lazzaro."

"I know," said Florida, with a faint blush.

"And yet, don't you see, it was as much a fancy of mine, a weakness for the man himself, as the desire to serve your mother, that prompted me to bring him to you."

"Yes, I see," answered the young girl.

"I acted in the teeth of a bitter Venetian prejudice against priests. All my friends here—they're mostly young men with the modern Italian ideas, or old liberals—hate and despise the priests They believe that priests are full of guile and deceit, that they are spies for the Austrians, and altogether evil."

"Don Ippolito is welcome to report our most secret thoughts to the police," said Florida, whose look of rising alarm relaxed into a smile.

"Oh," cried the painter, "how you leap to conclusions! I never intimated that Don Ippolito was a spy. On the contrary, it was his difference from other priests that made me think of him for a moment. He seems to be as much cut off from the church as from the world. And yet he is a priest, with a priest's education. What if I should have been altogether mistaken? He is either one of the openest souls in the world, as you have insisted, or he is one of the closest."

"I should not be afraid of him in any case," said Florida; "but I can't believe any wrong of him."

Ferris frowned in annoyance. "I don't want you to; I don't, myself. I've bungled the matter as I might have known I would. I was trying to put into words an undefined uneasiness of mine, a quite formless desire to have you possessed of the whole case as it had come up in my mind. I've made a mess of it," said Ferris rising, with a rueful air. "Besides, I ought to have spoken to Mrs. Vervain."

"Oh no," cried Florida, eagerly, springing to her feet beside him. "Don't! Little things wear upon my mother, so. I'm glad you didn't speak to her. I don't misunderstand you, I think; I expressed myself badly," she added with an anxious face. "I thank you very much. What do you want me to do?"

By Ferris's impulse they both began to move down the garden path toward the water-gate. The sunset had faded out of the fountain, but it still lit the whole heaven, in whose vast blue depths hung light whiffs of pinkish cloud, as ethereal as the draperies that floated after Miss Vervain as she walked with a splendid grace beside him, no awkwardness, now, or self-constraint in her. As she turned to Ferris, and asked in her deep tones, to which some latent feeling imparted a slight tremor, "What do you want me to do?" the sense of her willingness to be bidden by him gave him a delicious thrill. He looked at the superb creature, so proud, so helpless; so much a woman, so much a child; and he caught his breath before he answered. Her gauzes blew about his feet in the light breeze that lifted the foliage; she was a little near-sighted, and in her eagerness she drew closer to him, fixing her eyes full upon his with a bold innocence. "Good heavens!

Miss Vervain," he cried, with a sudden blush, "it isn't a serious matter. I'm a fool to have spoken to you. Don't do anything. Let things go on as before. It isn't for me to instruct you."

"I should have been very glad of your advice," she said with a disappointed, almost wounded manner, keeping her eyes upon him. "It seems to me we are always going wrong"—

She stopped short, with a flush and then a pallor.

Ferris returned her look with one of comical dismay. This apparent readiness of Miss Vervain's to be taken command of, daunted him, on second thoughts. "I wish you'd dismiss all my stupid talk from your mind," he said. "I feel as if I'd been guiltily trying to set you against a man whom I like very much and have no reason not to trust, and who thinks me so much his friend that he couldn't dream of my making any sort of trouble for him. It would break his heart, I'm afraid, if you treated him in a different way from that in which you've treated him till now. It's really touching to listen to his gratitude to you and your mother. It's only conceivable on the ground that he has never had friends before in the world. He seems like another man, or the same man come to life. And it isn't his fault that he's a priest. I suppose," he added, with a sort of final throe, "that a Venetian family wouldn't use him with the frank hospitality you've shown, not because they distrusted him at all, perhaps, but because they would be afraid of other Venetian tongues."

This ultimate drop of venom, helplessly distilled, did not seem to rankle in Miss Vervain's mind. She walked now with her face turned from his, and she answered coldly, "We shall not be troubled. We don't care for Venetian tongues."

They were at the gate. "Good-by," said Ferris, abruptly, "I'm going."

"Won't you wait and see my mother?" asked Florida, with her awkward self-constraint again upon her.

"No, thanks," said Ferris, gloomily. "I haven't time. I just dropped in for a moment, to blast an innocent man's reputation, and destroy a young lady's peace of mind."

"Then you needn't go, yet," answered Florida, coldly, "for you haven't succeeded."

"Well, I've done my worst," returned Ferris, drawing the bolt.

He went away, hanging his head in amazement and disgust at himself for his clumsiness and bad taste. It seemed to him a contemptible part, first to embarrass them with Don Ippolito's acquaintance, if it was an embarrassment, and then try to sneak out of his responsibility by these tardy cautions; and if it was not going to be an embarrassment, it was folly to have approached the matter at all.

What had he wanted to do, and with what motive? He hardly knew. As he battled the ground over and over again, nothing comforted him save the thought that, bad as it was to have spoken to Miss Vervain, it must have been infinitely worse to speak to her mother.

VIII

It was late before Ferris forgot his chagrin in sleep, and when he woke the next morning, the sun was making the solid green blinds at his window odorous of their native pine woods with its heat, and thrusting a golden spear at the heart of Don Ippolito's effigy where he had left it on the easel.

Marina brought a letter with his coffee. The letter was from Mrs. Vervain, and it entreated him to come to lunch at twelve, and then join them on an excursion, of which they had all often talked, up the Canal of the Brenta. "Don Ippolito has got his permission—think of his not being able to go to the mainland without the Patriarch's leave! and can go with us to-day. So I try to make this hasty arrangement. You *must* come—it all depends upon you."

"Yes, so it seems," groaned the painter, and went.

In the garden he found Don Ippolito and Florida, at the fountain where he had himself parted with her the evening before; and he observed with a guilty relief that Don Ippolito was talking to her in the happy unconsciousness habitual with him.

Florida cast at the painter a swift glance of latent appeal and intelligence, which he refused, and in the same instant she met him with another look, as if she now saw him for the first time, and gave him her hand in greeting. It was a beautiful hand; he could not help worshipping its lovely forms, and the lily whiteness and softness of the back, the rose of the palm and finger-tips.

She idly resumed the great Venetian fan which hung from her waist by a chain. "Don Ippolito has been talking about the vitteggiatura on the Brenta in the old days," she explained.

"Oh, yes," said the painter, "they used to have merry times in the villas then, and it was worth while being a priest, or at least an abbate di casa. I should think you would sigh for a return of those good old days, Don Ippolito. Just imagine, if you were abbate di casa with some patrician family about the close of the last century, you might be the instructor, companion, and spiritual adviser of Illustrissima at the theatres, card-parties, and masquerades, all winter; and at this season, instead of going up the Brenta for a day's pleasure with us barbarous Yankees, you might be setting out with Illustrissima and all the 'Strissimi and 'Strissime, big and little, for a spring villeggiatura there. You would be going in a gilded barge, with songs and fiddles and dancing, instead of a common gondola, and you would stay a month, walking, going to parties and caffes, drinking chocolate and lemonade gaming, sonneteering, and butterflying about generally."

"It was doubtless a beautiful life," answered the priest, with simple indifference. "But I never have thought of it with regret, because I have been preoccupied with other ideas than those of social pleasures, though perhaps they were no wiser."

Florida had watched Don Ippolito's face while Ferris was

speaking, and she now asked gravely, "But don't you think their life nowadays is more becoming to the clergy?"

"Why, madamigella? What harm was there in those gayeties? I suppose the bad features of the old life are exaggerated to us."

"They couldn't have been worse than the amusements of the hard-drinking, hard-riding, hard-swearing, fox-hunting English parsons about the same time," said Ferris. "Besides, the abbate di casa had a charm of his own, the charm of all *rococo* things, which, whatever you may say of them, are somehow elegant and refined, or at least refer to elegance and refinement. I don't say they're ennobling, but they're fascinating. I don't respect them, but I love them. When I think about the past of Venice, I don't care so much to see any of the heroically historical things; but I should like immensely to have looked in at the Ridotto, when the place was at its gayest with wigs and masks, hoops and small-clothes, fans and rapiers, bows and courtesies, whispers and glances. I dare say I should have found Don Ippolito there in some becoming disguise."

Florida looked from the painter to the priest and back to the painter, as Ferris spoke, and then she turned a little anxiously toward the terrace, and a shadow slipped from her face as her mother came rustling down the steps, catching at her drapery and shaking it into place. The young girl hurried to meet her, lifted her arms for what promised an embrace, and with firm hands set the elder lady's bonnet straight with her forehead.

"I'm always getting it on askew," Mrs. Vervain said for greeting to Ferris. "How do you do, Don Ippolito? But I suppose you think I've kept you long enough to get it on straight for once. So I have. I *am* a fuss, and I don't deny it. At my time of life, it's much harder to make yourself shipshape than it is when you're younger. I tell Florida that anybody would take *her* for the *old* lady, she does seem to give so little care to getting up an appearance."

"And yet she has the effect of a stylish young person in the bloom of youth," observed Ferris, with a touch of caricature.

"We had better lunch with our things on," said Mrs. Vervain, "and then there needn't be any delay in starting. I thought we would have it here," she added, as Nina and the house-servant appeared with trays of dishes and cups. "So that we can start in a real picnicky spirit. I knew you'd think it a womanish lunch, Mr. Ferris—Don Ippolito likes what we do—and so I've provided you with a chicken salad; and I'm going to ask you for a taste of it; I'm really hungry."

There was salad for all, in fact; and it was quite one o'clock before the lunch was ended, and wraps of just the right thickness and thinness were chosen, and the party were comfortably placed under the striped linen canopy of the gondola, which they had from a public station, the house-gondola being engaged that day. They rowed through the narrow canal skirting the garden out into the expanse before the Giudecca, and then struck across the lagoon towards Fusina, past the island-church of San Giorgio in Alga, whose beautiful tower has flushed and darkened in so many pictures of Venetian sunsets, and past the Austrian lagoon forts with their coronets of guns threatening every point, and the Croatian sentinels pacing to and fro on their walls. They stopped long enough at one of the customs barges to declare to the swarthy, amiable officers the innocence of their freight, and at the mouth of the Canal of the Brenta they paused before the station while a policeman came out and scanned them. He bowed to Don Ippolito's cloth, and then they began to push up the sluggish canal, shallow and overrun with weeds and mosses, into the heart of the land.

The spring, which in Venice comes in the softening air and the perpetual azure of the heavens, was renewed to their senses in all its miraculous loveliness. The garden of the Vervains had indeed confessed it in opulence of leaf and bloom, but there it seemed somehow only like a novel effect of the artifice which had been able to create a garden in that city of stone and sea. Here a vernal world suddenly opened before them, with wide-stretching fields of green under a dome of perfect blue; against its walls only the soft curves of far-off hills were traced, and near at hand the tender forms of full-foliaged trees. The long garland of vines that festoons all Italy seemed to begin in the neighboring orchards; the meadows waved their tall grasses in the sun, and broke in poppies as the sea-waves break in iridescent spray; the well-grown maize shook its gleaming blades in the light; the poplars marched in stately procession on either side of the straight, white road to Padua, till they vanished in the long perspective. The blossoms had fallen from the trees many weeks before, but the air was full of the vague sweetness of the perfect spring, which here and there gathered and defined itself as the spicy odor of the grass cut on the shore of the canal, and drying in the mellow heat of the sun.

The voyagers spoke from time to time of some peculiarity of the villas that succeeded each other along the canal. Don Ippolito knew a few of them, the gondoliers knew others; but after all, their names were nothing. These haunts of old-time splendor and idleness weary of themselves, and unable to escape, are sadder than anything in Venice, and they belonged, as far as the Americans were concerned, to a world as strange as any to which they should go in another life,—the world of a faded fashion and an alien history. Some of the villas were kept in a sort of repair; some were even maintained in the state of old; but the most showed marks of greater or less decay, and here and there one was falling to ruin. They had gardens about them, tangled and wild-grown; a population of decrepit statues in the rococo taste strolled in their walks or simpered from their gates. Two or three houses seemed to be occupied; the rest stood empty, each

"Close latticed to the brooding heat,
And silent in its dusty vines."

The pleasure-party had no fixed plan for the day further than to ascend the canal, and by and by take a carriage at some convenient village and drive to the famous Villa Pisani at Stra.

"These houses are very well," said Don Ippolito, who had visited the villa once, and with whom it had remained a memory almost as signal as that night in Padua when he wore civil dress, "but it is at Stra you see something really worthy of the royal splendor of the patricians of Venice. Royal? The villa is now one of the palaces of the ex-Emperor of Austria, who does not find it less imperial than his other palaces." Don Ippolito had celebrated the villa at Stra in this strain ever since they had spoken of going up the Brenta: now it was the magnificent conservatories and orangeries that he sang, now the vast garden with its statued walks between rows of clipt cedars and firs, now the stables with their stalls for numberless horses, now the palace itself with its frescoed halls and treasures of art and vertu. His enthusiasm for the villa at Stra had become an amiable jest with the Americans. Ferris laughed at his fresh outburst he declared himself tired of the gondola, and he asked Florida to disembark with him and walk under the trees of a pleasant street running on one side between the villas and the canal. "We are going to find something much grander than the Villa Pisani," he boasted, with a look at Don Ippolito.

As they sauntered along the path together, they came now

and then to a stately palace like that of the Contarini, where the lions, that give their name to one branch of the family, crouch in stone before the grand portal; but most of the houses were interesting only from their unstoried possibilities to the imagination. They were generally of stucco, and glared with fresh whitewash through the foliage of their gardens. When a peasant's cottage broke their line, it gave, with its barns and straw-stacks and its beds of pot-herbs, a homely relief from the decaying gentility of the villas.

"What a pity, Miss Vervain," said the painter, "that the blessings of this world should be so unequally divided! Why should all this sketchable adversity be lavished upon the neighborhood of a city that is so rich as Venice in picturesque dilapidation? It's pretty hard on us Americans, and forces people of sensibility into exile. What wouldn't cultivated persons give for a stretch of this street in the suburbs of Boston, or of your own Providence? I suppose the New Yorkers will be setting up something of the kind one of these days, and giving it a French name—they'll call it *Aux bords du Brenta*. There was one of them carried back a gondola the other day to put on a pond in their new park. But the worst of it is, you can't take home the sentiment of these things."

"I thought it was the business of painters to send home the sentiment of them in pictures," said Florida.

Ferris talked to her in this way because it was his way of talking; it always surprised him a little that she entered into the spirit of it; he was not quite sure that she did; he sometimes thought she waited till she could seize upon a point to turn against him, and so give herself the air of having comprehended the whole. He laughed: "Oh yes, a poor little fragmentary, faded-out reproduction of their sentiment—which is 'as moonlight unto sunlight and as water unto wine,' when compared with the real thing. Suppose I made a picture of this very bit, ourselves in the foreground, looking at the garden over there where that amusing Vandal of an owner has just had his statues painted white: would our friends at home understand it? A whole history must be left unexpressed. I could only hint at an entire situation. Of course, people with a taste for olives would get the flavor; but even they would wonder that I chose such an unsuggestive bit. Why, it is just the most maddeningly suggestive thing to be found here! And if I may put it modestly, for my share in it, I think we two young Americans looking on at this supreme excess of the rococo, are the very essence of the sentiment of the scene; but what would the honored connoisseurs—the good folks who get themselves up on Ruskin and try so honestly hard to have some little ideas about art—make of us? To be sure they might justifiably praise the grace of your pose, if I were so lucky as to catch it, and your way of putting your hand under the elbow of the arm that holds your parasol,"—Florida seemed disdainfully to keep her attitude, and the painter smiled,—"but they wouldn't know what it all meant, and couldn't imagine that we were inspired by this rascally little villa to sigh longingly over the wicked past."

"Excuse me," interrupted Florida, with a touch of trouble in her proud manner, "I'm not sighing over it, for one, and I don't want it back. I'm glad that I'm American and that there is no past for me. I can't understand how you and Don Ippolito can speak so tolerantly of what no one can respect," she added, in almost an aggrieved tone.

If Miss Vervain wanted to turn the talk upon Don Ippolito, Ferris by no means did; he had had enough of that subject yesterday; he got as lightly away from it as he could.

"Oh, Don Ippolito's a pagan, I tell you; and I'm a painter, and the rococo is my weakness. I wish I could paint it, but I can't; I'm a hundred years too late. I couldn't even paint myself in the act of sentimentalizing it."

While he talked, he had been making a few lines in a small pocket sketch-book, with a furtive glance or two at Florida. When they returned to the boat, he busied himself again with the book, and presently he handed it to Mrs. Vervain.

"Why, it's Florida!" cried the lady. "How very nicely you do sketch, Mr. Ferris."

"Thanks, Mrs. Vervain; you're always flattering me."

"No, but seriously. I *wish* that I had paid more attention to my drawing when I was a girl. And now, Florida—she won't touch a pencil. I wish you'd talk to her, Mr. Ferris."

"Oh, people who are pictures needn't trouble themselves to be painters," said Ferris, with a little burlesque.

Mrs. Vervain began to look at the sketch through her tubed hand; the painter made a grimace. "But you've made her too proud, Mr. Ferris. She doesn't look like that."

"Yes she does—to those unworthy of her kindness. I have taken Miss Vervain in the act of scorning the rococo, and its humble admirer, me, with it."

"I'm sure *I* don't know what you mean, Mr. Ferris; but I can't think that this proud look is habitual with Florida; and I've heard people say—very good judges—that an artist oughtn't to perpetuate a temporary expression. Something like that."

"It can't be helped now, Mrs. Vervain: the sketch is irretrievably immortal. I'm sorry, but it's too late."

"Oh, stuff! As if you couldn't turn up the corners of the mouth a little. Or something."

"And give her the appearance of laughing at me? Never!"

"Don Ippolito," said Mrs. Vervain, turning to the priest, who had been listening intently to all this trivial talk, "what do you think of this sketch?"

He took the book with an eager hand, and perused the sketch as if trying to read some secret there. After a minute he handed it back with a light sigh, apparently of relief, but said nothing.

"Well?" asked Mrs. Vervain.

"Oh! I ask pardon. No, it isn't my idea of madamigella. It seems to me that her likeness must be sketched in color. Those lines are true, but they need color to subdue them; they go too far, they are more than true."

"You're quite right, Don Ippolito," said Ferris.

"Then *you* don't think she always has this proud look?" pursued Mrs. Vervain. The painter fancied that Florida quelled in herself a movement of impatience; he looked at her with an amused smile.

"Not always, no," answered Don Ippolito.

"Sometimes her face expresses the greatest meekness in the world."

"But not at the present moment," thought Ferris, fascinated by the stare of angry pride which the girl bent upon the unconscious priest.

"Though I confess that I should hardly know how to characterize her habitual expression," added Don Ippolito.

"Thanks," said Florida, peremptorily. "I'm tired of the subject; it isn't an important one."

"Oh yes it is, my dear," said Mrs. Vervain. "At least it's important to me, if it isn't to you; for I'm your mother, and really, if I thought you looked like this, as a general thing, to a casual observer, I should consider it a reflection upon myself." Ferris gave a provoking laugh, as she continued sweetly, "I must insist, Don Ippolito: now did you ever see Florida look so?"

The girl leaned back, and began to wave her fan slowly to and fro before her face.

"I never saw her look so with you, dear madama," said the priest with an anxious glance at Florida, who let her fan fall folded into her lap, and sat still. He went on with priestly smoothness, and a touch of something like invoked authority, such as a man might show who could dispense indulgences and inflict penances. "No one could help seeing her devotedness to you, and I have admired from the first an obedience and tenderness that I have never known equaled. In all her relations to you, madamigella has seemed to me"—

Florida started forward. "You are not asked to comment on my behavior to my mother; you are not invited to speak of my conduct at all!" she burst out with sudden violence, her visage flaming, and her blue eyes burning upon Don Ippolito, who shrank from the astonishing rudeness as from a blow in the face. "What is it to you how I treat my mother?"

She sank back again upon the cushions, and opening the fan with a clash swept it swiftly before her.

"Florida!" said her mother gravely.

Ferris turned away in cold disgust, like one who has witnessed a cruelty done to some helpless thing. Don Ippolito's speech was not fortunate at the best, but it might have come from a foreigner's misapprehension, and at the worst it was good-natured and well-meant. "The girl is a perfect brute, as I thought in the beginning," the painter said to himself. "How could I have ever thought differently? I shall have to tell Don Ippolito that I'm ashamed of her, and disclaim all responsibility. Pah! I wish I was out of this."

The pleasure of the day was dead. It could not rally from that stroke. They went on to Stra, as they had planned, but the glory of the Villa Pisani was eclipsed for Don Ippolito. He plainly did not know what to do. He did not address Florida again, whose savagery he would not probably have known how to resent if he had wished to resent it. Mrs. Vervain prattled away to him with unrelenting kindness; Ferris kept near him, and with affectionate zeal tried to make him talk of the villa, but neither the frescoes, nor the orangeries, nor the green-houses, nor the stables, nor the gardens could rouse him from the listless daze in which he moved, though Ferris found them all as wonderful as he had said. Amidst this heavy embarrassment no one seemed at ease but the author of it. She did not, to be sure, speak to Don Ippolito, but she followed her mother as usual with her assiduous cares, and she appeared tranquilly unconscious of the sarcastic civility with which Ferris rendered her any service. It was late in the afternoon when they got back to their boat and began to descend the canal towards Venice, and long before they reached Fusina the day had passed. A sunset of melancholy red, streaked with level lines of murky cloud, stretched across the flats behind them, and faintly tinged with its reflected light the eastern horizon which the towers and domes of Venice had not yet begun to break. The twilight came, and then through the overcast heavens the moon shone dim; a light blossomed here and there in the villas, distant voices called musically; a cow lowed, a dog barked; the rich, sweet breath of the vernal land mingled its odors with the sultry air of the neighboring lagoon. The wayfarers spoke little; the time hung heavy on all, no doubt; to Ferris it was a burden almost intolerable to hear the creak of the oars and the breathing of the gondoliers keeping time together. At last the boat stopped in front of the police-station in Fusina; a soldier with a sword at his side and a lantern in his hand came out and briefly parleyed with the gondoliers; they stepped ashore, and he marched them into the station before him.

"We have nothing left to wish for now," said Ferris, breaking into an ironical laugh.

"What does it all mean?" asked Mrs. Vervain.

"I think I had better go see."

"We will go with you," said Mrs. Vervain.

"Pazienza!" replied Ferris.

The ladies rose; but Don Ippolito remained seated. "Aren't you going too, Don Ippolito?" asked Mrs. Vervain.

"Thanks, madama; but I prefer to stay here."

Lamentable cries and shrieks, as if the prisoners had imme-diately been put to the torture, came from the station as Ferris opened the door. A lamp of petroleum lighted the scene, and shone upon the figures of two fishermen, who bewailed themselves unintelligibly in the vibrant accents of Chiozza, and from time to time advanced upon the gondoliers, and shook their heads and beat their breasts at them, A few police-guards reclined upon benches about the room, and surveyed the spectacle with mild impassibility.

Ferris politely asked one of them the cause of the detention.

"Why, you see, signore," answered the guard amiably, "these honest men accuse your gondoliers of having stolen a rope out of their boat at Dolo."

"It was my blood, you know!" howled the elder of the fishermen, tossing his arms wildly abroad, "it was my own heart," he cried, letting the last vowel die away and rise again in mournful refrain, while he stared tragically into Ferris's face.

"What *is* the matter?" asked Mrs. Vervain, putting up her glasses, and trying with graceful futility to focus the melodrama.

"Nothing," said Ferris; "our gondoliers have had the heart's blood of this respectable Dervish; that is to say, they have stolen a rope belonging to him."

"*Our* gondoliers! I don't believe it. They've no right to keep us here all night. Tell them you're the American consul."

"I'd rather not try my dignity on these underlings, Mrs. Vervain; there's no American squadron here that I could order to bombard Fusina, if they didn't mind me. But I'll see what I can do further in quality of courteous foreigner. Can you perhaps tell me how long you will be obliged to detain us here?" he asked of the guard again.

"I am very sorry to detain you at all, signore. But what can I do? The commissary is unhappily absent. He may be here soon."

The guard renewed his apathetic contemplation of the gondoliers, who did not speak a word; the windy lamentation of the fishermen rose and fell fitfully. Presently they went out of doors and poured forth their wrongs to the moon.

The room was close, and with some trouble Ferris persuaded Mrs. Vervain to return to the gondola, Florida seconding his arguments with gentle good sense.

It seemed a long time till the commissary came, but his coming instantly simplified the situation. Perhaps because he had never been able to befriend a consul in trouble before, he befriended Ferris to the utmost. He had met him with rather a browbeating air; but after a glance at his card, he gave a kind of roar of deprecation and apology. He had the ladies and Don Ippolito in out of the gondola, and led them to an upper chamber, where he made them all repose their honored persons upon his sofas. He ordered up his housekeeper to make them coffee, which he served with his own hands, excusing its hurried feebleness, and he stood by, rubbing his palms together and smiling, while they refreshed themselves.

"They need never tell me again that the Austrians are tyrants," said Mrs. Vervain in undertone to the consul.

It was not easy for Ferris to remind his host of the malefactors; but he brought himself to this ungraciousness. The commissary begged pardon, and asked him to accompany him below, where he confronted the accused and the accusers. The tragedy was acted over again with blood-curdling effectiveness by the Chiozzotti; the gondoliers maintaining the calm of conscious innocence.

Ferris felt outraged by the trumped-up charge against them.

"Listen, you others the prisoners," said the commissary. "Your padrone is anxious to return to Venice, and I wish to inflict no further displeasures upon him. Restore their rope to these honest men, and go about your business."

The injured gondoliers spoke in low tones together; then one of them shrugged his shoulders and went out. He came back in a moment and laid a rope before the commissary.

"Is that the rope?" he asked. "We found it floating down the canal, and picked it up that we might give it to the rightful owner. But now I wish to heaven we had let it sink to the bottom of the sea."

"Oh, a beautiful story!" wailed the Chiozzoti. They flung themselves upon the rope, and lugged it off to their boat; and the gondoliers went out, too.

The commissary turned to Ferris with an amiable smile. "I am sorry that those rogues should escape," said the American.

"Oh," said the Italian, "they are poor fellows it is a little matter; I am glad to have served you."

He took leave of his involuntary guests with effusion, following them with a lantern to the gondola.

Mrs. Vervain, to whom Ferris gave an account of this trial as they set out again on their long-hindered return, had no mind save for the magical effect of his consular quality upon the commissary, and accused him of a vain and culpable modesty.

"Ah," said the diplomatist, "there's nothing like knowing just when to produce your dignity. There are some officials who know too little,—like those guards; and there are some who know too much,—like the commissary's superiors. But he is just in that golden mean of ignorance where he supposes a consul is a person of importance."

Mrs. Vervain disputed this, and Ferris submitted in silence. Presently, as they skirted the shore to get their bearings for the route across the lagoon, a fierce voice in Venetian shouted from the darkness, "Indrio, indrio!" (Back, back!) and a gleam of the moon through the pale, watery clouds revealed the figure of a gendarme on the nearest point of land. The gondoliers bent to their oars, and sent the boat swiftly out into the lagoon.

"There, for example, is a person who would be quite insensible to my greatness, even if I had the consular seal in my pocket. To him we are possible smugglers; [Footnote: Under the Austrians, Venice was a free port but everything carried there to the mainland was liable to duty.] and I must say," he continued, taking out his watch, and staring hard at it, "that if I were a disinterested person, and heard his suspicion met with the explanation that we were a little party out here for pleasure at half past twelve P. M., I should say he was right. At any rate we won't engage him in controversy. Quick, quick!" he added to the gondoliers, glancing at the receding shore, and then at the first of the lagoon forts which they were approaching. A dim shape moved along the top of the wall, and seemed to linger and scrutinize them. As they drew nearer, the challenge, "*Wer da?*" rang out.

The gondoliers eagerly answered with the one word of German known to their craft, "*Freunde*," and struggled to urge the boat forward; the oar of the gondolier in front slipped from the high rowlock, and fell out of his hand into the water. The gondola lurched, and then suddenly ran aground on the shallow. The sentry halted, dropped his gun from his shoulder, and ordered them to go on, while the gondoliers clamored back in the high key of fear, and one of them screamed out to his passengers to do something, saying that, a few weeks before, a sentinel had fired upon a fisherman and killed him.

"What's that he's talking about?" demanded Mrs. Vervain. "If we don't get on, it will be that man's duty to fire on us; he has no choice," she said, nerved and interested by the presence of this danger.

The gondoliers leaped into the water and tried to push the boat off. It would not move, and without warning, Don Ippolito, who had sat silent since they left Fusina, stepped over the side of the gondola, and thrusting an oar under its bottom lifted it free of the shallow.

"Oh, how very unnecessary!" cried Mrs. Vervain, as the priest and the gondoliers clambered back into the boat. "He will take his death of cold."

"It's ridiculous," said Ferris. "You ought to have told these worthless rascals what to do, Don Ippolito. You've got yourself wet for nothing. It's too bad!"

"It's nothing," said Don Ippolito, taking his seat on the little prow deck, and quietly dripping where the water would not incommode the others.

"Oh, here!" cried Mrs. Vervain, gathering some shawls together, "make him wrap those about him. He'll die, I know he will—with that reeking skirt of his. If you must go into the water, I wish you had worn your abbate's dress. How *could* you, Don Ippolito?"

The gondoliers set their oars, but before they had given a

W. D. Howells

stroke, they were arrested by a sharp "Halt!" from the fort. Another figure had joined the sentry, and stood looking at them.

"Well," said Ferris, "*now* what, I wonder? That's an officer. If I had a little German about me, I might state the situation to him."

He felt a light touch on his arm. "I can speak German," said Florida timidly.

"Then you had better speak it now," said Ferris.

She rose to her feet, and in a steady voice briefly explained the whole affair. The figures listened motionless; then the last comer politely replied, begging her to be in no uneasiness, made her a shadowy salute, and vanished. The sentry resumed his walk, and took no further notice of them.

"Brava!" said Ferris, while Mrs. Vervain babbled her satisfaction, "I will buy a German Ollendorff to-morrow. The language is indispensable to a pleasure excursion in the lagoon."

Florida made no reply, but devoted herself to restoring her mother to that state of defense against the discomforts of the time and place, which the common agitation had impaired. She seemed to have no sense of the presence of any one else. Don Ippolito did not speak again save to protect himself from the anxieties and reproaches of Mrs. Vervain, renewed and reiterated at intervals. She drowsed after a while, and whenever she woke she thought they had just touched her own landing. By fits it was cloudy and moonlight; they began to meet peasants' boats going to the Rialto market; at last, they entered the Canal of the Zattere, then they slipped into a narrow way, and presently stopped at Mrs. Vervain's gate; this time she had not expected it. Don Ippolito gave her his hand, and entered the garden with her, while Ferris lingered behind with Florida, helping her put together the wraps strewn about the gondola.

"Wait!" she commanded, as they moved up the garden walk. "I want to speak with you about Don Ippolito. What shall I do to him for my rudeness? You *must* tell me—you *shall*," she said in a fierce whisper, gripping the arm which Ferris had given to help her up the landing-stairs. "You are—older than I am!"

"Thanks. I was afraid you were going to say wiser. I should think your own sense of justice, your own sense of"—

"Decency. Say it, say it!" cried the girl passionately; "it was indecent, indecent—that was it!"

—"would tell you what to do," concluded the painter dryly.

She flung away the arm to which she had been clinging, and ran to where the priest stood with her mother at the foot of the terrace stairs. "Don Ippolito," she cried, "I want to tell you that I am sorry; I want to ask your pardon—how can you ever forgive me?—for what I said."

She instinctively stretched her hand towards him.

"Oh!" said the priest, with an indescribable long, trembling sigh. He caught her hand in his held it tight, and then pressed it for an instant against his breast.

Ferris made a little start forward.

"Now, that's right, Florida," said her mother, as the four stood in the pale, estranging moonlight. "I'm sure Don

Ippolito can't cherish any resentment. If he does, he must come in and wash it out with a glass of wine—that's a good old fashion. I want you to have the wine at any rate, Don Ippolito; it'll keep you from taking cold. You really must."

"Thanks, madama; I cannot lose more time, now; I must go home at once. Good night."

Before Mrs. Vervain could frame a protest, or lay hold of him, he bowed and hurried out of the land-gate.

"How perfectly absurd for him to get into the water in that way," she said, looking mechanically in the direction in which he had vanished.

"Well, Mrs. Vervain, it isn't best to be too grateful to people," said Ferris, "but I think we must allow that if we were in any danger, sticking there in the mud, Don Ippolito got us out of it by putting his shoulder to the oar."

"Of course," assented Mrs. Vervain.

"In fact," continued Ferris, "I suppose we may say that, under Providence, we probably owe our lives to Don Ippolito's self-sacrifice and Miss Vervain's knowledge of German. At any rate, it's what I shall always maintain."

"Mother, don't you think you had better go in?" asked Florida, gently. Her gentleness ignored the presence, the existence of Ferris. "I'm afraid you will be sick after all this fatigue."

"There, Mrs. Vervain, it'll be no use offering *me* a glass of wine. I'm sent away, you see," said Ferris. "And Miss Vervain is quite right. Good night."

"Oh—*good* night, Mr. Ferris," said Mrs. Vervain, giving her hand. "Thank you so much."

Florida did not look towards him. She gathered her mother's shawl about her shoulders for the twentieth time that day, and softly urged her in doors, while Ferris let himself out into the campo.

IX

Florida began to prepare the bed for her mother's lying down.

"What are you doing that for, my dear?" asked Mrs. Vervain. "I can't go to bed at once."

"But mother"—

"No, Florida. And I mean it. You are too headstrong. I should think you would see yourself how you suffer in the end by giving way to your violent temper. What a day you have made for us!"

"I was very wrong," murmured the proud girl, meekly.

"And then the mortification of an apology; you might have spared yourself that."

"It didn't mortify me; I didn't care for it."

"No, I really believe you are too haughty to mind humbling yourself. And Don Ippolito had been so uniformly kind to us. I begin to believe that Mr. Ferris caught your true character in that sketch. But your pride will be broken some day, Florida."

"Won't you let me help you undress, mother? You can talk to me while you're undressing. You must try to get some rest."

"Yes, I am all unstrung. Why couldn't you have let him come in and talk awhile? It would have been the best way to get me quieted down. But no; you must always have your own way Don't twitch me, my dear; I'd rather undress myself. You pretend to be very careful of me. I wonder if you really care for me."

"Oh, mother, you are all I have in the world!"

Mrs. Vervain began to whimper. "You talk as if I were any better off. Have I anybody besides you? And I have lost so many."

"Don't think of those things now, mother."

Mrs. Vervain tenderly kissed the young girl. "You are good to your mother. Don Ippolito was right; no one ever saw you offer me disrespect or unkindness. There, there! Don't cry, my darling. I think I *had* better lie down, and I'll let you undress me."

She suffered herself to be helped into bed, and Florida went softly about the room, putting it in order, and drawing the curtains closer to keep out the near dawn. Her mother talked a little while, and presently fell from incoherence to silence, and so to sleep.

Florida looked hesitatingly at her for a moment, and then set her candle on the floor and sank wearily into an arm-chair beside the bed. Her hands fell into her lap; her head drooped sadly forward; the light flung the shadow of her face grotesquely exaggerated and foreshortened upon the ceiling.

By and by a bird piped in the garden; the shriek of a swallow made itself heard from a distance; the vernal day was beginning to stir from the light, brief drowse of the vernal night. A crown of angry red formed upon the candle wick, which toppled over in the socket and guttered out with a sharp hiss.

Florida started from her chair. A streak of sunshine pierced shutter and curtain. Her mother was supporting herself on one elbow in the bed, and looking at her as if she had just called to her.

"Mother, did you speak?" asked the girl.

Mrs. Vervain turned her face away; she sighed deeply, stretched her thin hands on the pillow, and seemed to be sinking, sinking down through the bed. She ceased to breathe and lay in a dead faint.

Florida felt rather than saw it all. She did not cry out nor call for help. She brought water and cologne, and bathed her mother's face, and then chafed her hands. Mrs. Vervain slowly revived; she opened her eyes, then closed them; she did not speak, but after a while she began to fetch her breath with the long and even respirations of sleep.

Florida noiselessly opened the door, and met the servant with a tray of coffee. She put her finger to her lip, and motioned her not to enter, asking in a whisper: "What time is it, Nina? I forgot to wind my watch."

"It's nine o'clock, signorina; and I thought you would be tired this morning, and would like your coffee in bed. Oh, misericordia!" cried the girl, still in whisper, with a glance through the doorway, "you haven't been in bed at all!"

"My mother doesn't seem well. I sat down beside her, and fell asleep in my chair without knowing it."

"Ah, poor little thing! Then you must drink your coffee at once. It refreshes."

"Yes, yes," said Florida, closing the door, and pointing to a table in the next room, "put it down here. I will serve myself, Nina. Go call the gondola, please. I am going out, at once, and I want you to go with me. Tell Checa to come here and stay with my mother till I come back."

She poured out a cup of coffee with a trembling hand, and hastily drank it; then bathing her eyes, she went to the glass and bestowed a touch or two upon yesterday's toilet, studied the effect a moment, and turned away. She ran back for another look, and the next moment she was walking down to the water-gate, where she found Nina waiting her in the gondola.

A rapid course brought them to Ferris's landing. "Ring," she said to the gondolier, "and say that one of the American ladies wishes to see the consul."

Ferris was standing on the balcony over her, where he had been watching her approach in mute wonder. "Why, Miss Vervain," he called down, "what in the world is the matter?"

"I don't know. I want to see you," said Florida, looking up with a wistful face.

"I'll come down."

"Yes, please. Or no, I had better come up. Yes, Nina and I will come up."

Ferris met them at the lower door and led them to his apartment. Nina sat down in the outer room, and Florida followed the painter into his studio. Though her face was so wan, it seemed to him that he had never seen it lovelier, and he had a strange pride in her being there, though the disorder of the place ought to have humbled him. She looked over it with a certain childlike, timid curiosity, and something of that lofty compassion with which young ladies regard the haunts of men when they come into them by chance; in doing this she had a haughty, slow turn of the head that fascinated him.

"I hope," he said, "you don't mind the smell," which was a mingled one of oil-colors and tobacco-smoke. "The woman's putting my office to rights, and it's all in a cloud of dust. So I have to bring you in here."

Florida sat down on a chair fronting the easel, and found herself looking into the sad eyes of Don Ippolito. Ferris brusquely turned the back of the canvas toward her. "I didn't mean you to see that. It isn't ready to show, yet," he said, and then he stood expectantly before her. He waited for her to speak, for he never knew how to take Miss Vervain; he was willing enough to make light of her grand moods, but now she was too evidently unhappy for mocking; at the same time he did not care to invoke a snub by a prematurely sympathetic demeanor. His mind ran on the events of the day before, and he thought this visit probably related somehow to Don Ippolito. But his visitor did not speak, and at last he said: "I hope there's nothing wrong at home, Miss Vervain. It's rather odd to have yesterday, last night, and next morning all run together as they have been for me in the last twenty-four hours. I trust Mrs. Vervain is turning the whole thing into a good solid oblivion."

"It's about—it's about—I came to see you"—said Florida,

hoarsely. "I mean," she hurried on to say, "that I want to ask you who is the best doctor here?"

Then it was not about Don Ippolito. "Is your mother sick?" asked Ferris, eagerly. "She must have been fearfully tired by that unlucky expedition of ours. I hope there's nothing serious?"

"No, no! But she is not well. She is very frail, you know. You must have noticed how frail she is," said Florida, tremulously.

Ferris had noticed that all his countrywomen, past their girlhood, seemed to be sick, he did not know how or why; he supposed it was all right, it was so common. In Mrs. Vervain's case, though she talked a great deal about her ill-health, he had noticed it rather less than usual, she had so great spirit. He recalled now that he *had* thought her at times rather a shadowy presence, and that occasionally it had amused him that so slight a structure should hang together as it did—not only successfully, but triumphantly.

He said yes, he knew that Mrs. Vervain was not strong, and Florida continued: "It's only advice that I want for her, but I think we had better see some one—or know some one that we could go to in need. We are so far from any one we know, or help of any kind." She seemed to be trying to account to herself, rather than to Ferris, for what she was doing. "We mustn't let anything pass unnoticed".... She looked at him entreatingly, but a shadow, as of some wounding memory, passed over her face, and she said no more.

"I'll go with you to a doctor's," said Ferris, kindly.

"No, please, I won't trouble you."

"It's no trouble."

"I don't *want* you to go with me, please. I'd rather go alone." Ferris looked at her perplexedly, as she rose. "Just give me the address, and I shall manage best by myself. I'm used to doing it."

"As you like. Wait a moment." Ferris wrote the address. "There," he said, giving it to her; "but isn't there anything I can do for you?"

"Yes," answered Florida with awkward hesitation, and a half-defiant, half-imploring look at him. "You must have all sorts of people applying to you, as a consul; and you look after their affairs—and try to forget them"—

"Well?" said Ferris.

"I wish you wouldn't remember that I've asked this favor of you; that you'd consider it a"—

"Consular service? With all my heart," answered Ferris, thinking for the third or fourth time how very young Miss Vervain was.

"You are very good; you are kinder than I have any right," said Florida, smiling piteously. "I only mean, don't speak of it to my mother. Not," she added, "but what I want her to know everything I do; but it would worry her if she thought I was anxious about her. Oh! I wish I wouldn't."

She began a hasty search for her handkerchief; he saw her lips tremble and his soul trembled with them.

In another moment, "Good-morning," she said briskly, with a sort of airy sob, "I don't want you to come down, please."

She drifted out of the room and down the stairs, the servant-maid falling into her wake.

Ferris filled his pipe and went out on his balcony again, and stood watching the gondola in its course toward the address he had given, and smoking thoughtfully. It was really the same girl who had given poor Don Ippolito that cruel slap in the face, yesterday. But that seemed no more out of reason than her sudden, generous, exaggerated remorse both were of a piece with her coming to him for help now, holding him at a distance, flinging herself upon his sympathy, and then trying to snub him, and breaking down in the effort. It was all of a piece, and the piece was bad; yes, she had an ugly temper; and yet she had magnanimous traits too. These contradictions, which in his reverie he felt rather than formulated, made him smile, as he stood on his balcony bathed by the morning air and sunlight, in fresh, strong ignorance of the whole mystery of women's nerves. These caprices even charmed him. He reflected that he had gone on doing the Vervains one favor after another in spite of Florida's childish petulancies; and he resolved that he would not stop now; her whims should be nothing to him, as they had been nothing, hitherto. It is flattering to a man to be indispensable to a woman so long as he is not obliged to it; Miss Vervain's dependent relation to himself in this visit gave her a grace in Ferris's eyes which she had wanted before.

In the mean time he saw her gondola stop, turn round, and come back to the canal that bordered the Vervain garden.

"Another change of mind," thought Ferris, complacently; and rising superior to the whole fitful sex, he released himself from uneasiness on Mrs. Vervain's account. But in the evening he went to ask after her. He first sent his card to Florida, having written on it, "I hope Mrs. Vervain is better.

Don't let me come in if it's any disturbance." He looked for a moment at what he had written, dimly conscious that it was patronizing, and when he entered he saw that Miss Vervain stood on the defensive and from some willfulness meant to make him feel that he was presumptuous in coming; it did not comfort him to consider that she was very young. "Mother will be in directly," said Florida in a tone that relegated their morning's interview to the age of fable.

Mrs. Vervain came in smiling and cordial, apparently better and not worse for yesterday's misadventures.

"Oh, I pick up quickly," she explained. "I'm an old campaigner, you know. Perhaps a little *too* old, now. Years do make a difference; and you'll find it out as you get on, Mr. Ferris."

"I suppose so," said Ferris, not caring to have Mrs. Vervain treat him so much like a boy. "Even at twenty-six I found it pleasant to take a nap this afternoon. How does one stand it at seventeen, Miss Vervain?" he asked.

"I haven't felt the need of sleep," replied Florida, indifferently, and he felt shelved, as an old fellow.

He had an empty, frivolous visit, to his thinking. Mrs. Vervain asked if he had seen Don Ippolito, and wondered that the priest had not come about, al day. She told a long story, and at the end tapped herself on the mouth with her fan to punish a yawn.

Ferris rose to go. Mrs. Vervain wondered again in the same words why Don Ippolito had not been near them all day.

"Because he's a wise man," said Ferris with bitterness, "and knows when to time his visits." Mrs. Vervain did not notice his bitterness, but something made Florida follow him to the outer door.

"Why, it's moonlight!" she exclaimed; and she glanced at him as though she had some purpose of atonement in her mind.

But he would not have it. "Yes, there's a moon," he said moodily. "Good-night."

"Good night," answered Florida, and she impulsively offered him her hand. He thought that it shook in his, but it was probably the agitation of his own nerves.

A soreness that had been lifted from his heart, came back; he walked home disappointed and defeated, he hardly knew why or in what. He did not laugh now to think how she had asked him that morning to forget her coming to him for help; he was outraged that he should have been repaid in this sort, and the rebuff with which his sympathy had just been met was vulgar; there was no other name for it but vulgarity. Yet he could not relate this quality to the face of the young girl as he constantly beheld it in his homeward walk. It did not defy him or repulse him; it looked up at him wistfully as from the gondola that morning. Nevertheless he hardened his heart. The Vervains should see him next when they had sent for him. After all, one is not so very old at twenty-six.

X

"Don Ippolito has come, signorina," said Nina, the next morning, approaching Florida, where she sat in an attitude of listless patience, in the garden.

"Don Ippolito!" echoed the young girl in a weary tone. She rose and went into the house, and they met with the constraint which was but too natural after the events of their last parting. It is hard to tell which has most to overcome in such a case, the forgiver or the forgiven. Pardon rankles even in a generous soul, and the memory of having pardoned embarrasses the sensitive spirit before the object of its clemency, humbling and making it ashamed. It would be well, I suppose, if there need be nothing of the kind between human creatures, who cannot sustain such a relation without mutual distrust. It is not so ill with them when apart, but when they meet they must be cold and shy at first.

"Now I see what you two are thinking about," said Mrs. Vervain, and a faint blush tinged the cheek of the priest as she thus paired him off with her daughter. "You are thinking about what happened the other day; and you had better forget it. There is no use brooding over these matters. Dear me! if *I* had stopped to brood over every little unpleasant thing that happened, I wonder where I should be now? By the way, where were *you* all day yesterday, Don Ippolito?"

"I did not come to disturb you because I thought you must be very tired. Besides I was quite busy."

"Oh yes, those inventions of yours. I think you are *so* ingenious! But you mustn't apply too closely. Now really, yesterday,— after all you had been through, it was too much for the brain." She tapped herself on the forehead with her fan.

"I was not busy with my inventions, madama," answered Don Ippolito, who sat in the womanish attitude priests get from their drapery, and fingered the cord round his three-cornered hat. "I have scarcely touched them of late. But our parish takes part in the procession of Corpus Domini in the Piazza, and I had my share of the preparations."

"Oh, to be sure! When is it to be? We must all go. Our Nina has been telling Florida of the grand sights,—little children dressed up like John the Baptist, leading lambs. I suppose it's a great event with you."

The priest shrugged his shoulders, and opened both his hands, so that his hat slid to the floor, bumping and tumbling some distance away. He recovered it and sat down again. "It's an observance," he said coldly.

"And shall you be in the procession?"

"I shall be there with the other priests of my parish."

"Delightful!" cried Mrs. Vervain. "We shall be looking out for you. I shall feel greatly honored to think I actually know some one in the procession. I'm going to give you a little nod. You won't think it very wrong?"

She saved him from the embarrassment he might have felt in

replying, by an abrupt lapse from all apparent interest in the subject. She turned to her daughter, and said with a querulous accent, "I wish you would throw the afghan over my feet, Florida, and make me a little comfortable before you begin your reading this morning." At the same time she feebly disposed herself among the sofa cushions on which she reclined, and waited for some final touches from her daughter. Then she said, "I'm just going to close my eyes, but I shall hear every word. You are getting a beautiful accent, my dear, I know you are. I should think Goldoni must have a very smooth, agreeable style; hasn't he now, in Italian?"

They began to read the comedy; after fifteen or twenty minutes Mrs. Vervain opened her eyes and said, "But before you commence, Florida, I wish you'd play a little, to get me quieted down. I feel so very flighty. I suppose it's this sirocco. And I believe I'll lie down in the next room."

Florida followed her to repeat the arrangements for her comfort. Then she returned, and sitting down at the piano struck with a sort of soft firmness a few low, soothing chords, out of which a lulling melody grew. With her fingers still resting on the keys she turned her stately head, and glanced through the open door at her mother.

"Don Ippolito," she asked softly, "is there anything in the air of Venice that makes people very drowsy?"

"I have never heard that, madamigella."

"I wonder," continued the young girl absently, "why my mother wants to sleep so much."

"Perhaps she has not recovered from the fatigues of the other night," suggested the priest.

"Perhaps," said Florida, sadly looking toward her mother's door.

She turned again to the instrument, and let her fingers wander over the keys, with a drooping head. Presently she lifted her face, and smoothed back from her temples some straggling tendrils of hair. Without looking at the priest she asked with the child-like bluntness that characterized her, "Why don't you like to walk in the procession of Corpus Domini?"

Don Ippolito's color came and went, and he answered evasively, "I have not said that I did not like to do so."

"No, that is true," said Florida, letting her fingers drop again on the keys.

Don Ippolito rose from the sofa where he had been sitting beside her while they read, and walked the length of the room. Then he came towards her and said meekly, "Madamigella, I did not mean to repel any interest you feel in me. But it was a strange question to ask a priest, as I remembered I was when you asked it."

"Don't you always remember that?" demanded the girl, still without turning her head.

"No; sometimes I am suffered to forget it," he said with a tentative accent.

She did not respond, and he drew a long breath, and walked away in silence. She let her hands fall into her lap, and sat in an attitude of expectation. As Don Ippolito came near her again he paused a second time.

"It is in this house that I forget my priesthood," he began, "and it is the first of your kindnesses that you suffer me to do so, your good mother, there, and you. How shall I repay you? It cut me to the heart that you should ask forgiveness of me when you did, though I was hurt by your rebuke. Oh, had you not the right to rebuke me if I abused the delicate unreserve with which you had always treated me? But believe me, I meant no wrong, then."

His voice shook, and Florida broke in, "You did nothing wrong. It was I who was cruel for no cause."

"No, no. You shall not say that," he returned. "And why should I have cared for a few words, when all your acts had expressed a trust of me that is like heaven to my soul?"

She turned now and looked at him, and he went on. "Ah, I see you do not understand! How could you know what it is to be a priest in this most unhappy city? To be haunted by the strict espionage of all your own class, to be shunned as a spy by all who are not of it! But you two have not put up that barrier which everywhere shuts me out from my kind. You have been willing to see the man in me, and to let me forget the priest."

"I do not know what to say to you, Don Ippolito. I am only a foreigner, a girl, and I am very ignorant of these things," said Florida with a slight alarm. "I am afraid that you may be saying what you will be sorry for."

"Oh never! Do not fear for me if I am frank with you. It is my refuge from despair."

The passionate vibration of his voice increased, as if it must break in tears. She glanced towards the other room with a little movement or stir.

"Ah, you needn't be afraid of listening to me!" cried the priest bitterly.

"I will not wake her," said Florida calmly, after an instant.

"See how you speak the thing you mean, always, always, always! You could not deny that you meant to wake her, for you have the life-long habit of the truth. Do you know what it is to have the life-long habit of a lie? It is to be a priest. Do you know what it is to seem, to say, to do, the thing you are not, think not, will not? To leave what you believe unspoken, what you will undone, what you are unknown? It is to be a priest!"

Don Ippolito spoke in Italian, and he uttered these words in a voice carefully guarded from every listener but the one before his face. "Do you know what it is when such a moment as this comes, and you would fling away the whole fabric of falsehood that has clothed your life—do you know what it is to keep still so much of it as will help you to unmask silently and secretly? It is to be a priest!"

His voice had lost its vehemence, and his manner was strangely subdued and cold. The sort of gentle apathy it expressed, together with a certain sad, impersonal surprise at the difference between his own and the happier fortune with which he contrasted it, was more touching than any tragic demonstration.

As if she felt the fascination of the pathos which she could not fully analyze, the young girl sat silent. After a time, in which she seemed to be trying to think it all out, she asked in a low, deep murmur: "Why did you become a priest, then?"

"It is a long story," said Don Ippolito. "I will not trouble you with it now. Some other time."

"No; now," answered Florida, in English. "If you hate so to be a priest, I can't understand why you should have allowed yourself to become one. We should be very unhappy if we could not respect you,—not trust you as we have done; and how could we, if we knew you were not true to yourself in being what you are?"

"Madamigella," said the priest, "I never dared believe that I was in the smallest thing necessary to your happiness. Is it true, then, that you care for my being rather this than that? That you are in the least grieved by any wrong of mine?"

"I scarcely know what you mean. How could we help being grieved by what you have said to me?"

"Thanks; but why do you care whether a priest of my church loves his calling or not,—you, a Protestant? It is that you are sorry for me as an unhappy man, is it not?"

"Yes; it is that and more. I am no Catholic, but we are both Christians"—

Don Ippolito gave the faintest movement of his shoulders.

—"and I cannot endure to think of your doing the things you must do as a priest, and yet hating to be a priest. It is terrible!"

"Are all the priests of your faith devotees?"

"They cannot be. But are none of yours so?"

"Oh, God forbid that I should say that. I have known real saints among them. That friend of mine in Padua, of whom I once told you, became such, and died an angel fit for Paradise. And I suppose that my poor uncle is a saint, too, in his way."

"Your uncle? A priest? You have never mentioned him to us."

"No," said Don Ippolito. After a certain pause he began abruptly, "We are of the people, my family, and in each generation we have sought to honor our blood by devoting one of the race to the church. When I was a child, I used to divert myself by making little figures out of wood and pasteboard, and I drew rude copies of the pictures I saw at church. We lived in the house where I live now, and where I was born, and my mother let me play in the small chamber where I now have my forge; it was anciently the oratory of the noble family that occupied the whole palace. I contrived an altar at one end of it; I stuck my pictures about the walls, and I ranged the puppets in the order of worshippers on the floor; then I played at saying mass, and preached to them all day long.

"My mother was a widow. She used to watch me with tears in her eyes. At last, one day, she brought my uncle to see me: I remember it all far better than yesterday. 'Is it not the will of God?' she asked. My uncle called me to him, and asked me whether I should like to be a priest in good earnest, when I grew up? 'Shall I then be able to make as many little figures as I like, and to paint pictures, and carve an altar like that in your church?' I demanded. My uncle answered that I should have real men and women to preach to, as he had, and would not that be much finer? In my heart I did not think so, for I did not care for that part of it; I only liked to preach to my puppets because I had made them. But said, 'Oh yes,' as children do. I kept on contriving the toys that I played with, and I grew used to hearing it told among my mates and about the neighborhood that I was to be a priest; I cannot remember any other talk with my mother, and I do not know

W. D. Howells

how or when it was decided. Whenever I thought of the matter, I thought, 'That will be very well. The priests have very little to do, and they gain a great deal of money with their masses; and I shall be able to make whatever I like.' I only considered the office then as a means to gratify the passion that has always filled my soul for inventions and works of mechanical skill and ingenuity. My inclination was purely secular, but I was as inevitably becoming a priest as if I had been born to be one."

"But you were not forced? There was no pressure upon you?"

"No, there was merely an absence, so far as they were concerned, of any other idea. I think they meant justly, and assuredly they meant kindly by me. I grew in years, and the time came when I was to begin my studies. It was my uncle's influence that placed me in the Seminary of the Salute, and there I repaid his care by the utmost diligence. But it was not the theological studies that I loved, it was the mathematics and their practical application, and among the classics I loved best the poets and the historians. Yes, I can see that I was always a mundane spirit, and some of those in charge of me at once divined it, I think. They used to take us to walk,—you have seen the little creatures in their priest's gowns, which they put on when they enter the school, with a couple of young priests at the head of the file,—and once, for an uncommon pleasure, they took us to the Arsenal, and let us see the shipyards and the museum. You know the wonderful things that are there: the flags and the guns captured from the Turks; the strange weapons of all devices; the famous suits of armor. I came back half-crazed; I wept that I must leave the place. But I set to work the best I could to carve out in wood an invention which the model of one of the antique galleys had suggested to me. They found it,— nothing can be concealed outside of your own breast in such a school,—and they carried me with my contrivance before the superior. He looked kindly but gravely at me: 'My son,' said he, 'do you wish to be a priest?' 'Surely, reverend father,' I answered in alarm, 'why not?' 'Because these things are not for priests. Their thoughts must be upon other things. Consider well of it, my son, while there is yet time,' he said, and he addressed me a long and serious discourse upon the life on which I was to enter. He was a just and conscientious and affectionate man; but every word fell like burning fire in my heart. At the end, he took my poor plaything, and thrust it down among the coals of his *scaldino*. It made the scaldino smoke, and he bade me carry it out with me, and so turned again to his book.

"My mother was by this time dead, but I could hardly have gone to her, if she had still been living. 'These things are not for priests!' kept repeating itself night and day in my brain. I was in despair, I was in a fury to see my uncle. I poured out my heart to him, and tried to make him understand the illusions and vain hopes in which I had lived. He received coldly my sorrow and the reproaches which I did not spare him; he bade me consider my inclinations as so many temptations to be overcome for the good of my soul and the glory of God. He warned me against the scandal of attempting to withdraw now from the path marked out for me. I said that I never would be a priest. 'And what will you do?' he asked. Alas! what could I do? I went back to my prison, and in due course I became a priest.

"It was not without sufficient warning that I took one order after another, but my uncle's words, 'What will you do?' made me deaf to these admonitions. All that is now past. I no longer resent nor hate; I seem to have lost the power; but those were days when my soul was filled with bitterness. Something of this must have showed itself to those who had me in their charge. I have heard that at one time my superiors had grave doubts whether I ought to be allowed to take orders. My examination, in which the difficulties of the sacerdotal life were brought before me with the greatest clearness, was severe; I do not know how I passed it; it must have been in grace to my uncle. I spent the next ten days in a convent, to meditate upon the step I was about to take. Poor helpless, friendless wretch! Madamigella, even yet I cannot see how I was to blame, that I came forth and received the first of the holy orders, and in their time the second and the third.

"I was a priest, but no more a priest at heart than those Venetian conscripts, whom you saw carried away last week, are Austrian soldiers. I was bound as they are bound, by an inexorable and inevitable law.

"You have asked me why I became a priest. Perhaps I have not told you why, but I have told you how—I have given you the slight outward events, not the processes of my mind— and that is all that I can do. If the guilt was mine, I have suffered for it. If it was not mine, still I have suffered for it. Some ban seems to have rested upon whatever I have attempted. My work,—oh, I know it well enough!—has all been cursed with futility; my labors are miserable failures or contemptible successes. I have had my unselfish dreams of blessing mankind by some great discovery or invention; but my life has been barren, barren, barren; and save for the kindness that I have known in this house, and that would not let me despair, it would now be without hope."

He ceased, and the girl, who had listened with her proud looks transfigured to an aspect of grieving pity, fetched a long sigh. "Oh, I am sorry for you!" she said, "more sorry than I know how to tell. But you must not lose courage, you must not give up!"

Don Ippolito resumed with a melancholy smile. "There are doubtless temptations enough to be false under the best of conditions in this world. But something—I do not know what or whom; perhaps no more my uncle or my mother than I, for they were only as the past had made them—caused me to begin by living a lie, do you not see?"

"Yes, yes," reluctantly assented the girl.

"Perhaps—who knows?—that is why no good has come of me, nor can come. My uncle's piety and repute have always been my efficient help. He is the principal priest of the church to which I am attached, and he has had infinite patience with me. My ambition and my attempted inventions are a scandal to him, for he is a priest of those like the Holy Father, who believe that all the wickedness of the modern world has come from the devices of science; my indifference to the things of religion is a terror and a sorrow to him which he combats with prayers and penances. He starves himself and goes cold and faint that God may have mercy and turn my heart to the things on which his own is fixed. He loves my soul, but not me, and we are scarcely friends."

Florida continued to look at him with steadfast, compassionate eyes. "It seems very strange, almost like some dream," she murmured, "that you should be saying all this to me, Don Ippolito, and I do not know why I should have asked you anything."

The pity of this virginal heart must have been very sweet to the man on whom she looked it. His eyes worshipped her, as he answered her devoutly, "It was due to the truth in you that I should seem to you what I am."

"Indeed, you make me ashamed!" she cried with a blush. "It was selfish of me to ask you to speak. And now, after what you have told me, I am so helpless and I know so very little that I don't understand how to comfort or encourage you. But surely you can somehow help yourself. Are men, that seem so strong and able, just as powerless as women, after all, when it comes to real trouble? Is a man"—

"I cannot answer. I am only a priest," said Don Ippolito coldly, letting his eyes drop to the gown that fell about him like a woman's skirt.

"Yes, but a priest should be a man, and so much more; a priest"—

Don Ippolito shrugged his shoulders.

"No, no!" cried the girl. "Your own schemes have all failed, you say; then why do you not think of becoming a priest in reality, and getting the good there must be in such a calling? It is singular that I should venture to say such a thing to you, and it must seem presumptuous and ridiculous for me, a Protestant—but our ways are so different."... She paused, coloring deeply, then controlled herself, and added with grave composure, "If you were to pray"—

"To what, madamigella?" asked the priest, sadly.

"To what!" she echoed, opening her eyes full upon him. "To God!"

Don Ippolito made no answer. He let his head fall so low upon his breast that she could see the sacerdotal tonsure.

"You must excuse me," she said, blushing again. "I did not mean to wound your feelings as a Catholic. I have been very bold and intrusive. I ought to have remembered that people of your church have different ideas—that the saints"—

Don Ippolito looked up with pensive irony.

"Oh, the poor saints!"

"I don't understand you," said Florida, very gravely.

"I mean that I believe in the saints as little as you do."

"But you believe in your Church?"

"I have no Church."

There was a silence in which Don Ippolito again dropped his head upon his breast. Florida leaned forward in her eagerness, and murmured, "You believe in God?"

The priest lifted his eyes and looked at her beseechingly. "I do not know," he whispered. She met his gaze with one of dumb bewilderment. At last she said: "Sometimes you baptize little children and receive them into the church in the name of God?"

"Yes."

"Poor creatures come to you and confess their sins, and you absolve them, or order them to do penances?"

"Yes."

"And sometimes when people are dying, you must stand by their death-beds and give them the last consolations of religion?"

"It is true."

"Oh!" moaned the girl, and fixed on Don Ippolito a long look of wonder and reproach, which he met with eyes of silent anguish.

"It is terrible, madamigella," he said, rising. "I know it. I would fain have lived single-heartedly, for I think I was made so; but now you see how black and deadly a lie my life is. It is worse than you could have imagined, is it not? It is worse than the life of the cruelest bigot, for he at least believes in himself."

"Worse, far worse!"

"But at least, dear young lady," he went on piteously, "believe me that I have the grace to abhor myself. It is not much, it is very, very little, but it is something. Do not wholly condemn me!"

"Condemn? Oh, I am sorry for you with my whole heart. Only, why must you tell me all this? No, no; you are not to blame. I made you speak; I made you put yourself to shame."

"Not that, dearest madamigella. I would unsay nothing now, if I could, unless to take away the pain I have given you. It has been more a relief than a shame to have all this known to you; and even if you should despise me"—

"I don't despise you; that isn't for me; but oh, I wish that I could help you!"

Don Ippolito shook his head. "You cannot help me; but I thank you for your compassion; I shall never forget it." He lingered irresolutely with his hat in his hand. "Shall we go on with the reading, madamigella?"

"No, we will not read any more to-day," she answered.

"Then I relieve you of the disturbance, madamigella," he said; and after a moment's hesitation he bowed sadly and went.

She mechanically followed him to the door, with some little gestures and movements of a desire to keep him from going, yet let him go, and so turned back and sat down with her hands resting noiseless on the keys of the piano.

XI

The next morning Don Ippolito did not come, but in the afternoon the postman brought a letter for Mrs. Vervain, couched in the priest's English, begging her indulgence until after the day of Corpus Christi, up to which time, he said, he should be too occupied for his visits of ordinary.

This letter reminded Mrs. Vervain that they had not seen Mr. Ferris for three days, and she sent to ask him to dinner. But he returned an excuse, and he was not to be had to breakfast the next morning for the asking. He was in open rebellion. Mrs. Vervain had herself rowed to the consular landing, and sent up her gondolier with another invitation to dinner.

The painter appeared on the balcony in the linen blouse which he wore at his work, and looked down with a frown on the smiling face of Mrs. Vervain for a moment without speaking. Then, "I'll come," he said gloomily.

"Come with me, then," returned Mrs. Vervain,

"I shall have to keep you waiting."

"I don't mind that. You'll be ready in five minutes."

Florida met the painter with such gentleness that he felt his resentment to have been a stupid caprice, for which there was no ground in the world. He tried to recall his fading sense of outrage, but he found nothing in his mind but penitence. The sort of distraught humility with which she behaved gave her a novel fascination.

The dinner was good, as Mrs. Vervain's dinners always were, and there was a compliment to the painter in the presence of a favorite dish. When he saw this, "Well, Mrs. Vervain, what is it?" he asked. "You needn't pretend that you're treating me so well for nothing. You want something."

"We want nothing but that you should not neglect your friends. We have been utterly deserted for three or four days. Don Ippolito has not been here, either; but *he* has some excuse; he has to get ready for Corpus Christi. He's going to be in the procession."

"Is he to appear with his flying machine, or his portable dining-table, or his automatic camera?"

"For shame!" cried Mrs. Vervain, beaming reproach. Florida's face clouded, and Ferris made haste to say that he did not know these inventions were sacred, and that he had no wish to blaspheme them.

"You know well enough what I meant," answered Mrs. Vervain. "And now, we want you to get us a window to look out on the procession."

"Oh, *that's* what you want, is it? I thought you merely wanted me not to neglect my friends."

"Well, do you call that neglecting them?"

"Mrs. Vervain, Mrs. Vervain! What a mind you have! Is

there anything else you want? Me to go with you, for example?"

"We don't insist. You can take us to the window and leave us, if you like."

"This clemency is indeed unexpected," replied Ferris. "I'm really quite unworthy of it."

He was going on with the badinage customary between Mrs. Vervain and himself, when Florida protested,—

"Mother, I think we abuse Mr. Ferris's kindness."

"I know it, my dear—I know it," cheerfully assented Mrs. Vervain. "It's perfectly shocking. But what are we to do? We must abuse *somebody's* kindness."

"We had better stay at home. I'd much rather not go," said the girl, tremulously.

"Why, Miss Vervain," said Ferris gravely, "I'm very sorry if you've misunderstood my joking. I've never yet seen the procession to advantage, and I'd like very much to look on with you."

He could not tell whether she was grateful for his words, or annoyed. She resolutely said no more, but her mother took up the strain and discoursed long upon it, arranging all the particulars of their meeting and going together. Ferris was a little piqued, and began to wonder why Miss Vervain did not stay at home if she did not want to go. To be sure, she went everywhere with her mother but it was strange, with her habitual violent submissiveness, that she should have said anything in opposition to her mother's wish or purpose.

After dinner, Mrs. Vervain frankly withdrew for her nap, and Florida seemed to make a little haste to take some sewing in her hand, and sat down with the air of a woman willing; to detain her visitor. Ferris was not such a stoic as not to be dimly flattered by this, but he was too much of a man to be fully aware how great an advance it might seem.

"I suppose we shall see most of the priests of Venice, and what they are like, in the procession to-morrow," she said. "Do you remember speaking to me about priests, the other day, Mr. Ferris?"

"Yes, I remember it very well. I think I overdid it; and I couldn't perceive afterwards that I had shown any motive but a desire to make trouble for Don Ippolito."

"I never thought that," answered Florida, seriously. "What you said was true, wasn't it?"

"Yes, it was and it wasn't, and I don't know that it differed from anything else in the world, in that respect. It is true that there is a great distrust of the priests amongst the Italians. The young men hate them—or think they do—or say they do. Most educated men in middle life are materialists, and of course unfriendly to the priests. There are even women who are skeptical about religion. But I suspect that the largest number of all those who talk loudest against the priests are really subject to them. You must consider how very intimately they are bound up with every family in the most solemn relations of life."

"Do you think the priests are generally bad men?" asked the young girl shyly.

"I don't, indeed. I don't see how things could hang together if it were so. There must be a great basis of sincerity and goodness in them, when all is said and done. It seems to me that at the worst they're merely professional people—poor fellows who have gone into the church for a living. You know it isn't often now that the sons of noble families take orders; the priests are mostly of humble origin; not that they're necessarily the worse for that; the patricians used to be just as bad in another way."

"I wonder," said Florida, with her head on one side, considering her seam, "why there is always something so dreadful to us in the idea of a priest."

"They *do* seem a kind of alien creature to us Protestants. I can't make out whether they seem so to Catholics, or not. But we have a repugnance to all doomed people, haven't we? And a priest is a man under sentence of death to the natural ties between himself and the human race. He is dead to us. That makes him dreadful. The spectre of our dearest friend, father or mother, would be terrible. And yet," added Ferris, musingly, "a nun isn't terrible."

"No," answered the girl, "that's because a woman's life even in the world seems to be a constant giving up. No, a nun isn't unnatural, but a priest is."

She was silent for a time, in which she sewed swiftly; then she suddenly dropped her work into her lap, and pressing it down with both hands, she asked, "Do you believe that priests themselves are ever skeptical about religion?"

"I suppose it must happen now and then. In the best days of the church it was a fashion to doubt, you know. I've often wanted to ask our friend Don Ippolito something about these matters, but I didn't see how it could be managed." Ferris did not note the change that passed over Florida's face, and he continued. "Our acquaintance hasn't become so intimate as I hoped it might. But you only get to a certain point with Italians. They like to meet you on the street; maybe they haven't any indoors."

"Yes, it must sometimes happen, as you say," replied Florida, with a quick sigh, reverting to the beginning of Ferris's answer. "But is it any worse for a false priest than for a hypocritical minister?"

"It's bad enough for either, but it's worse for the priest. You see Miss Vervain, a minister doesn't set up for so much. He doesn't pretend to forgive us our sins, and he doesn't ask us to confess them; he doesn't offer us the veritable body and blood in the sacrament, and he doesn't bear allegiance to the visible and tangible vicegerent of Christ upon earth. A hypocritical parson may be absurd; but a skeptical priest is tragical."

"Yes, oh yes, I see," murmured the girl, with a grieving face. "Are they always to blame for it? They must be induced, sometimes, to enter the church before they've seriously thought about it, and then don't know how to escape from the path that has been marked out for them from their childhood. Should you think such a priest as that was to blame for being a skeptic?" she asked very earnestly.

"No," said Ferris, with a smile at her seriousness, "I should think such a skeptic as that was to blame for being a priest."

"Shouldn't you be very sorry for him?" pursued Florida still more solemnly.

"I should, indeed, if I liked him. If I didn't, I'm afraid I shouldn't," said Ferris; but he saw that his levity jarred upon her. "Come, Miss Vervain, you're not going to look at those fat monks and sleek priests in the procession to-morrow as so many incorporate tragedies, are you? You'll spoil my pleasure if you do. I dare say they'll be all of them devout believers, accepting everything, down to the animalcula in the holy water."

"If *you* were that kind of a priest," persisted the girl, without heeding his jests, "what should you do?"

"Upon my word, I don't know. I can't imagine it. Why," he continued, "think what a helpless creature a priest is in everything but his priesthood—more helpless than a woman, even. The only thing he could do would be to leave the church, and how could he do that? He's in the world, but he isn't of it, and I don't see what he could do with it, or it with him. If an Italian priest were to leave the church, even the liberals, who distrust him now, would despise him still more. Do you know that they have a pleasant fashion of calling the Protestant converts apostates? The first thing for such a priest would be exile. But I'm not supposably the kind of priest you mean, and I don't think just such a priest supposable. I dare say if a priest found himself drifting into doubt, he'd try to avoid the disagreeable subject, and, if he couldn't, he'd philosophize it some way, and wouldn't let his skepticism worry him."

"Then you mean that they haven't consciences like us?"

"They have consciences, but not like us. The Italians are kinder people than we are, but they're not so just, and I should say that they don't think truth the chief good of life. They believe there are pleasanter and better things. Perhaps they're right."

"No, no; you don't believe that, you know you don't," said Florida, anxiously. "And you haven't answered my question."

"Oh yes, I have. I've told you it wasn't a supposable case."

"But suppose it was."

"Well, if I must," answered Ferris with a laugh. "With my unfortunate bringing up, I couldn't say less than that such a man ought to get out of his priesthood at any hazard. He should cease to be a priest, if it cost him kindred, friends, good fame, country, everything. I don't see how there can be any living in such a lie, though I know there is. In all reason, it ought to eat the soul out of a man, and leave him helpless to do or be any sort of good. But there seems to be something, I don't know what it is, that is above all reason of ours, something that saves each of us for good in spite of the bad that's in us. It's very good practice, for a man who wants to be modest, to come and live in a Latin country. He learns to suspect his own topping virtues, and to be lenient to the novel combinations of right and wrong that he sees. But as for our insupposable priest—yes, I should say decidedly he ought to get out of it by all means."

Florida fell back in her chair with an aspect of such relief as comes to one from confirmation on an important point. She passed her hand over the sewing in her lap, but did not speak.

Ferris went on, with a doubting look at her, for he had been shy of introducing Don Ippolito's name since the day on the Brenta, and he did not know what effect a recurrence to him in this talk might have. "I've often wondered if our own clerical friend were not a little shaky in his faith. I don't think nature meant him for a priest. He always strikes me as an extremely secular-minded person. I doubt if he's ever put the question whether he is what he professes to be, squarely to himself—he's such a mere dreamer."

W. D. Howells

Florida changed her posture slightly, and looked down at her sewing. She asked, "But shouldn't you abhor him if he were a skeptical priest?"

Ferris shrugged his shoulders. "Oh, I don't find it such an easy matter to abhor people. It would be interesting," he continued musingly, "to have such a dreamer waked up, once, and suddenly confronted with what he recognized as perfect truthfulness, and couldn't help contrasting himself with. But it would be a little cruel."

"Would you rather have him left as he was?" asked Florida, lifting her eyes to his.

"As a moralist, no; as a humanitarian, yes, Miss Vervain. He'd be much happier as he was."

"What time ought we to be ready for you tomorrow?" demanded the girl in a tone of decision,

"We ought to be in the Piazza by nine o'clock," said Ferris, carelessly accepting the change of subject; and he told her of his plan for seeing the procession from a window of the Old Procuratie.

When he rose to go, he said lightly, "Perhaps, after all, we may see the type of tragical priest we've been talking about. Who can tell? I say his nose will be red."

"Perhaps," answered Florida, with unheeding gravity.

XII

The day was one of those which can come to the world only in early June at Venice. The heaven was without a cloud, but a blue haze made mystery of the horizon where the lagoon and sky met unseen. The breath of the sea bathed in freshness the city at whose feet her tides sparkled and slept.

The great square of St. Mark was transformed from a mart, from a *salon*, to a temple. The shops under the colonnades that inclose it upon three sides were shut; the caffes, before which the circles of idle coffee-drinkers and sherbet-eaters ordinarily spread out into the Piazza, were repressed to the limits of their own doors; the stands of the water-venders, the baskets of those that sold oranges of Palermo and black cherries of Padua, had vanished from the base of the church of St. Mark, which with its dim splendor of mosaics and its carven luxury of pillar and arch and finial rose like the high-altar, ineffably rich and beautiful, of the vaster temple whose inclosure it completed. Before it stood the three great red flag-staffs, like painted tapers before an altar, and from them hung the Austrian flags of red and white, and yellow and black.

In the middle of the square stood the Austrian military band, motionless, encircling their leader with his gold-headed staff uplifted. During the night a light colonnade of wood, roofed

W. D. Howells

with blue cloth, had been put up around the inside of the Piazza, and under this now paused the long pomp of the ecclesiastical procession—the priests of all the Venetian churches in their richest vestments, followed in their order by facchini, in white sandals and gay robes, with caps of scarlet, white, green, and blue, who bore huge painted candles and silken banners displaying the symbol or the portrait of the titular saints of the several churches, and supported the canopies under which the host of each was elevated. Before the clergy went a company of Austrian soldiers, and behind the facchini came a long array of religious societies, charity-school boys in uniforms, old paupers in holiday dress, little naked urchins with shepherds' crooks and bits of fleece about their loins like John the Baptist in the Wilderness, little girls with angels' wings and crowns, the monks of the various orders, and civilian penitents of all sorts in cloaks or dress-coats, hooded or bareheaded, and carrying each a lighted taper. The corridors under the Imperial Palace and the New and Old Procuratie were packed with spectators; from every window up and down the fronts of the palaces, gay stuffs were flung; the startled doves of St. Mark perched upon the cornices, or fluttered uneasily to and fro above the crowd. The baton of the band leader descended with a crash of martial music, the priests chanted, the charity-boys sang shrill, a vast noise of shuffling feet arose, mixed with the foliage-like rustling of the sheets of tinsel attached to the banners and candles in the procession: the whole strange, gorgeous picture came to life.

After all her plans and preparations, Mrs. Vervain had not felt well enough that morning to come to the spectacle which she had counted so much upon seeing, but she had therefore insisted the more that her daughter should go, and Ferris now stood with Florida alone at a window in the Old Procuratie.

"Well, what do you think, Miss Vervain?" he asked, when

their senses had somewhat accustomed themselves to the noise of the procession; "do you say now that Venice is too gloomy a city to have ever had any possibility of gayety in her?"

"I never said that," answered Florida, opening her eyes upon him.

"Neither did I," returned Ferris, "but I've often thought it, and I'm not sure now but I'm right. There's something extremely melancholy to me in all this. I don't care so much for what one may call the deplorable superstition expressed in the spectacle, but the mere splendid sight and the music are enough to make one shed tears. I don't know anything more affecting except a procession of lantern-lit gondolas and barges on the Grand Canal. It's phantasmal. It's the spectral resurrection of the old dead forms into the present. It's not even the ghost, it's the corpse, of other ages that's haunting Venice. The city ought to have been destroyed by Napoleon when he destroyed the Republic, and thrown overboard—St. Mark, Winged Lion, Bucentaur, and all. There is no land like America for true cheerfulness and light-heartedness. Think of our Fourth of Julys and our State Fairs. Selah!"

Ferris looked into the girl's serious face with twinkling eyes. He liked to embarrass her gravity with his antic speeches, and enjoyed her endeavors to find an earnest meaning in them, and her evident trouble when she could find none.

"I'm curious to know how our friend will look," he began again, as he arranged the cushion on the window-sill for Florida's greater comfort in watching the spectacle, "but it won't be an easy matter to pick him out in this masquerade, I fancy. Candle-carrying, as well as the other acts of devotion, seems rather out of character with Don Ippolito, and I can't imagine his putting much soul into it. However, very few of the clergy appear to do that. Look at those holy men with their eyes to the wind! They are wondering who is the *bella bionda* at the window here."

Florida listened to his persiflage with an air of sad distraction. She was intent upon the procession as it approached from the other side of the Piazza, and she replied at random to his comments on the different bodies that formed it.

"It's very hard to decide which are my favorites," he continued, surveying the long column through an operaglass. "My religious disadvantages have been such that I don't care much for priests or monks, or young John the Baptists, or small female cherubim, but I do like little charity-boys with voices of pins and needles and hair cut *a la* dead-rabbit. I should like, if it were consistent with the consular dignity, to go down and rub their heads. I'm fond, also, of *old* charity-boys, I find. Those paupers make one in love with destitute and dependent age, by their aspect of irresponsible enjoyment. See how briskly each of them topples along on the leg that he hasn't got in the grave! How attractive likewise are the civilian devotees in those imperishable dress-coats of theirs! Observe their high collars of the era of the Holy Alliance: they and their fathers and their grandfathers before them have worn those dress-coats; in a hundred years from now their posterity will keep holiday in them. I should like to know the elixir by which the dress-coats of civil employees render themselves immortal. Those penitents in the cloaks and cowls are not bad, either, Miss Vervain. Come, they add a very pretty touch of mystery to this spectacle. They're the sort of thing that painters are expected to paint in Venice—that people sigh over as so peculiarly Venetian. If you've a single sentiment about you, Miss Vervain, now is the time to produce it."

"But I haven't. I'm afraid I have no sentiment at all,"

answered the girl ruefully. "But this makes me dreadfully sad."

"Why that's just what I was saying a while ago. Excuse me, Miss Vervain, but your sadness lacks novelty; it's a sort of plagiarism."

"Don't, please," she pleaded yet more earnestly. "I was just thinking—I don't know why such an awful thought should come to me—that it might all be a mistake after all; perhaps there might not be any other world, and every bit of this power and display of the church—*our* church as well as the rest—might be only a cruel blunder, a dreadful mistake. Perhaps there isn't even any God! Do you think there is?"

"I don't *think* it," said Ferris gravely, "I *know* it. But I don't wonder that this sight makes you doubt. Great God! How far it is from Christ! Look there, at those troops who go before the followers of the Lamb: their trade is murder. In a minute, if a dozen men called out, 'Long live the King of Italy!' it would be the duty of those soldiers to fire into the helpless crowd. Look at the silken and gilded pomp of the servants of the carpenter's son! Look at those miserable monks, voluntary prisoners, beggars, aliens to their kind! Look at those penitents who think that they can get forgiveness for their sins by carrying a candle round the square! And it is nearly two thousand years since the world turned Christian! It is pretty slow. But I suppose God lets men learn Him from their own experience of evil. I imagine the kingdom of heaven is a sort of republic, and that God draws men to Him only through their perfect freedom."

"Yes, yes, it must be so," answered Florida, staring down on the crowd with unseeing eyes, "but I can't fix my mind on it. I keep thinking the whole time of what we were talking about yesterday. I never could have dreamed of a priest's disbelieving; but now I can't dream of anything else. It seems to me that none of these priests or monks can believe anything. Their faces look false and sly and bad—*all* of them!"

"No, no, Miss Vervain," said Ferris, smiling at her despair, "you push matters a little beyond—as a woman has a right to do, of course. I don't think their faces are bad, by any means. Some of them are dull and torpid, and some are frivolous, just like the faces of other people. But I've been noticing the number of good, kind, friendly faces, and they're in the majority, just as they are amongst other people; for there are very few souls altogether out of drawing, in my opinion. I've even caught sight of some faces in which there was a real rapture of devotion, and now and then a very innocent one. Here, for instance, is a man I should like to bet on, if he'd only look up."

The priest whom Ferris indicated was slowly advancing toward the space immediately under their window. He was dressed in robes of high ceremony, and in his hand he carried a lighted taper. He moved with a gentle tread, and the droop of his slender figure intimated a sort of despairing weariness. While most of his fellows stared carelessly or curiously about them, his face was downcast and averted.

Suddenly the procession paused, and a hush fell upon the vast assembly. Then the silence was broken by the rustle and stir of all those thousands going down upon their knees, as the cardinal-patriarch lifted his hands to bless them.

The priest upon whom Ferris and Florida had fixed their eyes faltered a moment, and before he knelt his next neighbor had to pluck him by the skirt. Then he too knelt hastily, mechanically lifting his head, and glancing along the front of the Old Procuratie. His face had that weariness in it which his figure and movement had suggested, and it was very pale, but it was yet more singular for the troubled innocence which its traits expressed.

"There," whispered Ferris, "that's what I call an uncommonly good face."

Florida raised her hand to silence him, and the heavy gaze of the priest rested on them coldly at first. Then a light of recognition shot into his eyes and a flush suffused his pallid visage, which seemed to grow the more haggard and desperate. His head fell again, and he dropped the candle from his hand. One of those beggars who went by the side of the procession, to gather the drippings of the tapers, restored it to him.

"Why," said Ferris aloud, "it's Don Ippolito! Did you know him at first?"

W. D. Howells

XIII

The ladies were sitting on the terrace when Don Ippolito came next morning to say that he could not read with Miss Vervain that day nor for several days after, alleging in excuse some priestly duties proper to the time. Mrs. Vervain began to lament that she had not been able to go to the procession of the day before. "I meant to have kept a sharp lookout for you; Florida saw you, and so did Mr. Ferris. But it isn't at all the same thing, you know. Florida has no faculty for describing; and now I shall probably go away from Venice without seeing you in your real character once."

Don Ippolito suffered this and more in meek silence. He waited his opportunity with unfailing politeness, and then with gentle punctilio took his leave.

"Well, come again as soon as your duties will let you, Don Ippolito," cried Mrs. Vervain. "We shall miss you dreadfully, and I begrudge every one of your readings that Florida loses."

The priest passed, with the sliding step which his impeding drapery imposed, down the garden walk, and was half-way to the gate, when Florida, who had stood watching him, said to her mother, "I must speak to him again," and lightly descended the steps and swiftly glided in pursuit.

"Don Ippolito!" she called.

He already had his hand upon the gate, but he turned, and rapidly went back to meet her.

She stood in the walk where she had stopped when her voice arrested him, breathing quickly. Their eyes met; a painful shadow overcast the face of the young girl, who seemed to be trying in vain to speak.

Mrs. Vervain put on her glasses and peered down at the two with good-natured curiosity.

"Well, madamigella," said the priest at last, "what do you command me?" He gave a faint, patient sigh.

The tears came into her eyes. "Oh," she began vehemently, "I wish there was some one who had the right to speak to you!"

"No one," answered Don Ippolito, "has so much the right as you."

"I saw you yesterday," she began again, "and I thought of what you had told me, Don Ippolito."

"Yes, I thought of it, too," answered the priest; "I have thought of it ever since."

"But haven't you thought of any hope for yourself? Must you still go on as before? How can you go back now to those things, and pretend to think them holy, and all the time have no heart or faith in them? It's terrible!"

"What would you, madamigella?" demanded Don Ippolito, with a moody shrug. "It is my profession, my trade, you know. You might say to the prisoner," he added bitterly, "'It is terrible to see you chained here.' Yes, it is terrible. Oh, I don't reject your compassion! But what can I do?"

"Sit down with me here," said Florida in her blunt, child-like way, and sank upon the stone seat beside the walk. She clasped her hands together in her lap with some strong, bashful emotion, while Don Ippolito, obeying her command, waited for her to speak. Her voice was scarcely more than a hoarse whisper when she began.

"I don't know how to begin what I want to say. I am not fit to advise any one. I am so young, and so very ignorant of the world."

"I too know little of the world," said the priest, as much to himself as to her.

"It may be all wrong, all wrong. Besides," she said abruptly, "how do I know that you are a good man, Don Ippolito? How do I know that you've been telling me the truth? It may be all a kind of trap"—

He looked blankly at her.

"This is in Venice; and you may be leading me on to say things to you that will make trouble for my mother and me. You may be a spy"—

"Oh no, no, no!" cried the priest, springing to his feet with a kind of moan, and a shudder, "God forbid!" He swiftly touched her hand with the tips of his fingers, and then kissed them: an action of inexpressible humility. "Madamigella, I swear to you by everything you believe good that I would rather die than be false to you in a single breath or thought."

"Oh, I know it, I know it," she murmured. "I don't see how I could say such a cruel thing."

"Not cruel; no, madamigella, not cruel," softly pleaded Don Ippolito.

"But—but is there *no* escape for you?"

They looked steadfastly at each other for a moment, and then Don Ippolito spoke.

"Yes," he said very gravely, "there is one way of escape. I have often thought of it, and once I thought I had taken the first step towards it; but it is beset with many great obstacles, and to be a priest makes one timid and insecure."

He lapsed into his musing melancholy with the last words; but she would not suffer him to lose whatever heart he had begun to speak with. "That's nothing," she said, "you must think again of that way of escape, and never turn from it till you have tried it. Only take the first step and you can go on. Friends will rise up everywhere, and make it easy for you. Come," she implored him fervently, "you must promise."

He bent his dreamy eyes upon her.

"If I should take this only way of escape, and it seemed desperate to all others, would you still be my friend?"

"I should be your friend if the whole world turned against you."

"Would you be my friend," he asked eagerly in lower tones, and with signs of an inward struggle, "if this way of escape were for me to be no longer a priest?"

"Oh yes, yes! Why not?" cried the girl; and her face glowed

with heroic sympathy and defiance. It is from this heaven-born ignorance in women of the insuperable difficulties of doing right that men take fire and accomplish the sublime impossibilities. Our sense of details, our fatal habits of reasoning paralyze us; we need the impulse of the pure ideal which we can get only from them. These two were alike children as regarded the world, but he had a man's dark prevision of the means, and she a heavenly scorn of every-thing but the end to be achieved.

He drew a long breath. "Then it does not seem terrible to you?"

"Terrible? No! I don't see how you can rest till it is done!"

"Is it true, then, that you urge me to this step, which indeed I have so long desired to take?"

"Yes, it is true! Listen, Don Ippolito: it is the very thing that I hoped you would do, but I wanted you to speak of it first. You must have all the honor of it, and I am glad you thought of it before. You will never regret it!"

She smiled radiantly upon him, and he kindled at her enthusiasm. In another moment his face darkened again. "But it will cost much," he murmured.

"No matter," cried Florida. "Such a man as you ought to leave the priesthood at any risk or hazard. You should cease to be a priest, if it cost you kindred, friends, good fame, country, everything!" She blushed with irrelevant conscious-ness. "Why need you be downhearted? With your genius once free, you can make country and fame and friends everywhere. Leave Venice! There are other places. Think how inventors succeed in America"—

"In America!" exclaimed the priest. "Ah, how long I have desired to be there!"

"You must go. You will soon be famous and honored there, and you shall not be a stranger, even at the first. Do you know that we are going home very soon? Yes, my mother and I have been talking of it to-day. We are both homesick, and you see that she is not well. You shall come to us there, and make our house your home till you have formed some plans of your own. Everything will be easy. God *is* good," she said in a breaking voice, "and you may be sure he will befriend you."

"Some one," answered Don Ippolito, with tears in his eyes, "has already been very good to me. I thought it was you, but I will call it God!"

"Hush! You mustn't say such things. But you must go, now. Take time to think, but not too much time. Only,—be true to yourself."

They rose, and she laid her hand on his arm with an instinctive gesture of appeal. He stood bewildered. Then, "Thanks, madamigella, thanks!" he said, and caught her fragrant hand to his lips. He loosed it and lifted both his arms by a blind impulse in which he arrested himself with a burning blush, and turned away. He did not take leave of her with his wonted formalities, but hurried abruptly toward the gate.

A panic seemed to seize her as she saw him open it. She ran after him. "Don Ippolito, Don Ippolito," she said, coming up to him; and stammered and faltered. "I don't know; I am frightened. You must do nothing from me; I cannot let you; I'm not fit to advise you. It must be wholly from your own conscience. Oh no, don't look so! I *will* be your friend, whatever happens. But if what you think of doing has seemed so terrible to you, perhaps it *is* more terrible than I can understand. If it is the only way, it is right. But is there no other? What I mean is, have you no one to talk all this over with? I mean, can't you speak of it to—to Mr. Ferris? He is so true and honest and just."

"I was going to him," said Don Ippolito, with a dim trouble in his face.

"Oh, I am so glad of that! Remember, I don't take anything back. No matter what happens, I will be your friend. But he will tell you just what to do."

Don Ippolito bowed and opened the gate.

Florida went back to her mother, who asked her, "What in the world have you and Don Ippolito been talking about so earnestly? What makes you so pale and out of breath?"

"I have been wanting to tell you, mother," said Florida. She drew her chair in front of the elder lady, and sat down.

XIV

Don Ippolito did not go directly to the painter's. He walked toward his house at first, and then turned aside, and wandered out through the noisy and populous district of Canaregio to the Campo di Marte. A squad of cavalry which had been going through some exercises there was moving off the parade ground; a few infantry soldiers were strolling about under the trees. Don Ippolito walked across the field to the border of the lagoon, where he began to pace to and fro, with his head sunk in deep thought. He moved rapidly, but sometimes he stopped and stood still in the sun, whose heat he did not seem to feel, though a perspiration bathed his pale face and stood in drops on his forehead under the shadow of his nicchio. Some little dirty children of the poor, with which this region swarms, looked at him from the sloping shore of the Campo di Giustizia, where the executions used to take place, and a small boy began to mock his movements and pauses, but was arrested by one of the girls, who shook him and gesticulated warningly.

At this point the long railroad bridge which connects Venice with the mainland is in full sight, and now from the reverie in which he continued, whether he walked or stood still, Don Ippolito was roused by the whistle of an outward train. He followed it with his eye as it streamed along over the far-stretching arches, and struck out into the flat, salt marshes

W. D. Howells

beyond. When the distance hid it, he put on his hat, which he had unknowingly removed, and turned his rapid steps toward the railroad station. Arrived there, he lingered in the vestibule for half an hour, watching the people as they bought their tickets for departure, and had their baggage examined by the customs officers, and weighed and registered by the railroad porters, who passed it through the wicket shutting out the train, while the passengers gathered up their smaller parcels and took their way to the waiting-rooms. He followed a group of English people some paces in this direction, and then returned to the wicket, through which he looked long and wistfully at the train. The baggage was all passed through; the doors of the waiting-rooms were thrown open with harsh proclamation by the guards, and the passengers flocked into the carriages. Whistles and bells were sounded, and the train crept out of the station.

A man in the company's uniform approached the unconscious priest, and striking his hands softly together, said with a pleasant smile, "Your servant, Don Ippolito. Are you expecting some one?"

"Ah, good day!" answered the priest, with a little start. "No," he added, "I was not looking for any one."

"I see," said the other. "Amusing yourself as usual with the machinery. Excuse the freedom, Don Ippolito; but you ought to have been of our profession,—ha, ha! When you have the leisure, I should like to show you the drawing of an American locomotive which a friend of mine has sent me from Nuova York. It is very different from ours, very curious. But monstrous in size, you know, prodigious! May I come with it to your house, some evening?"

"You will do me a great pleasure," said Don Ippolito. He gazed dreamily in the direction of the vanished train. "Was that the train for Milan?" he asked presently.

"Exactly," said the man.

"Does it go all the way to Milan?"

"Oh, no! it stops at Peschiera, where the passengers have their passports examined; and then another train backs down from Desenzano and takes them on to Milan. And after that," continued the man with animation, "if you are on the way to England, for example, another train carries you to Susa, and there you get the diligence over the mountain to St. Michel, where you take railroad again, and so on up through Paris to Boulogne-sur-Mer, and then by steamer to Folkestone, and then by railroad to London and to Liverpool. It is at Liverpool that you go on board the steamer for America, and piff! in ten days you are in Nuova York. My friend has written me all about it."

"Ah yes, your friend. Does he like it there in America?"

"Passably, passably. The Americans have no manners; but they are good devils. They are governed by the Irish. And the wine is dear. But he likes America; yes, he likes it. Nuova York is a fine city. But immense, you know! Eight times as large as Venice!"

"Is your friend prosperous there?"

"Ah heigh! That is the prettiest part of the story. He has made himself rich. He is employed by a large house to make designs for mantlepieces, and marble tables, and tombs; and he has—listen!—six hundred francs a month!"

"Oh per Bacco!" cried Don Ippolito.

"Honestly. But you spend a great deal there. Still, it is magnificent, is it not? If it were not for that blessed war there, now, that would be the place for you, Don Ippolito. He tells me the Americans are actually mad for inventions. Your servant. Excuse the freedom, you know," said the man, bowing and moving away.

"Nothing, dear, nothing," answered the priest. He walked out of the station with a light step, and went to his own house, where he sought the room in which his inventions were stored. He had not touched them for weeks. They were all dusty and many were cobwebbed. He blew the dust from some, and bringing them to the light, examined them critically, finding them mostly disabled in one way or other, except the models of the portable furniture which he polished with his handkerchief and set apart, surveying them from a distance with a look of hope. He took up the breech-loading cannon and then suddenly put it down again with a little shiver, and went to the threshold of the perverted oratory and glanced in at his forge. Veneranda had carelessly left the window open, and the draught had carried the ashes about the floor. On the cinder-heap lay the tools which he had used in mending the broken pipe of the fountain at Casa Vervain, and had not used since. The place seemed chilly even on that summer's day. He stood in the doorway with clenched hands. Then he called Veneranda, chid her for leaving the window open, and bade her close it, and so quitted the house and left her muttering.

Ferris seemed surprised to see him when he appeared at the consulate near the middle of the afternoon, and seated himself in the place where he was wont to pose for the painter.

"Were you going to give me a sitting?" asked the latter, hesitating. "The light is horrible, just now, with this glare from the canal. Not that I manage much better when it's good. I don't get on with you, Don Ippolito. There are too many of you. I shouldn't have known you in the procession yesterday."

Don Ippolito did not respond. He rose and went toward his portrait on the easel, and examined it long, with a curious minuteness. Then he returned to his chair, and continued to look at it. "I suppose that it resembles me a great deal," he said, "and yet I do not *feel* like that. I hardly know what is the fault. It is as I should be if I were like other priests, perhaps?"

"I know it's not good," said the painter. "It *is* conventional, in spite of everything. But here's that first sketch I made of you."

He took up a canvas facing the wall, and set it on the easel. The character in this charcoal sketch was vastly sincerer and sweeter.

"Ah!" said Don Ippolito, with a sigh and smile of relief, "that is immeasurably better. I wish I could speak to you, dear friend, in a mood of yours as sympathetic as this picture records, of some matters that concern me very nearly. I have just come from the railroad station."

"Seeing some friends off?" asked the painter, indifferently, hovering near the sketch with a bit of charcoal in his hand, and hesitating whether to give it a certain touch. He glanced with half-shut eyes at the priest.

Don Ippolito sighed again. "I hardly know. I was seeing off my hopes, my desires, my prayers, that followed the train to America!"

The painter put down his charcoal, dusted his fingers, and looked at the priest without saying anything.

"Do you remember when I first came to you?" asked Don Ippolito.

"Certainly," said Ferris. "Is it of that matter you want to speak to me? I'm very sorry to hear it, for I don't think it practical."

"Practical, practical!" cried the priest hotly. "Nothing is practical till it has been tried. And why should I not go to America?"

"Because you can't get your passport, for one thing," answered the painter dryly.

"I have thought of that," rejoined Don Ippolito more patiently. "I can get a passport for France from the Austrian authorities here, and at Milan there must be ways in which I could change it for one from my own king"—it was by this title that patriotic Venetians of those days spoke of Victor Emmanuel—"that would carry me out of France into England."

Ferris pondered a moment. "That is quite true," he said. "Why hadn't you thought of that when you first came to me?"

"I cannot tell. I didn't know that I could even get a passport for France till the other day."

Both were silent while the painter filled his pipe. "Well," he said presently, "I'm very sorry. I'm afraid you're dooming yourself to many bitter disappointments in going to America. What do you expect to do there?"

"Why, with my inventions"—

"I suppose," interrupted the other, putting a lighted match to his pipe, "that a painter must be a very poor sort of American: *his* first thought is of coming to Italy. So I know very little directly about the fortunes of my inventive fellow-countrymen, or whether an inventor has any prospect of making a living. But once when I was at Washington I went into the Patent Office, where the models of the inventions are deposited; the building is about as large as the Ducal Palace, and it is full of them. The people there told me nothing was commoner than for the same invention to be repeated over and over again by different inventors. Some few succeed, and then they have lawsuits with the infringers of their patents; some sell out their inventions for a trifle to companies that have capital, and that grow rich upon them; the great number can never bring their ideas to the public notice at all. You can judge for yourself what your chances would be. You have asked me why you should not go to America. Well, because I think you would starve there."

"I am used to that," said Don Ippolito; "and besides, until some of my inventions became known, I could give lessons in Italian."

"Oh, bravo!" said Ferris, "you prefer instant death, then?"

"But madamigella seemed to believe that my success as an inventor would be assured, there."

Ferris gave a very ironical laugh. "Miss Vervain must have been about twelve years old when she left America. Even a lady's knowledge of business, at that age, is limited. When did you talk with her about it? You had not spoken of it to me, of late, and I thought you were more contented than you used to be."

"It is true," said the priest. "Sometimes within the last two months I have almost forgotten it."

"And what has brought it so forcibly to your mind again?"

"That is what I so greatly desire to tell you," replied Don Ippolito, with an appealing look at the painter's face. He moistened his parched lips a little, waiting for further question from the painter, to whom he seemed a man fevered by some strong emotion and at that moment not quite wholesome. Ferris did not speak, and Don Ippolito began again: "Even though I have not said so in words to you, dear friend, has it not appeared to you that I have no heart in my vocation?"

"Yes, I have sometimes fancied that. I had no right to ask you why."

"Some day I will tell you, when I have the courage to go all over it again. It is partly my own fault, but it is more my miserable fortune. But wherever the wrong lies, it has at last become intolerable to me. I cannot endure it any longer and live. I must go away, I must fly from it."

Ferris shrank from him a little, as men instinctively do from one who has set himself upon some desperate attempt. "Do you mean, Don Ippolito, that you are going to renounce your priesthood?"

Don Ippolito opened his hands and let his priesthood drop, as it were, to the ground.

"You never spoke of this before, when you talked of going to America. Though to be sure"—

"Yes, yes!" replied Don Ippolito with vehemence, "but now

an angel has appeared and shown me the blackness of my life!"

Ferris began to wonder if he or Don Ippolito were not perhaps mad.

"An angel, yes," the priest went on, rising from his chair, "an angel whose immaculate truth has mirrored my falsehood in all its vileness and distortion—to whom, if it destroys me, I cannot devote less than a truthfulness like hers!"

"Hers—hers?" cried the painter, with a sudden pang. "Whose? Don't speak in these riddles. Whom do you mean?"

"Whom can I mean but only one?—madamigella!"

"Miss Vervain? Do you mean to say that Miss Vervain has advised you to renounce your priesthood?"

"In as many words she has bidden me forsake it at any risk,—at the cost of kindred, friends, good fame, country, everything."

The painter passed his hand confusedly over his face. These were his own words, the words he had used in speaking with Florida of the supposed skeptical priest. He grew very pale. "May I ask," he demanded in a hard, dry voice, "how she came to advise such a step?"

"I can hardly tell. Something had already moved her to learn from me the story of my life—to know that I was a man with neither faith nor hope. Her pure heart was torn by the thought of my wrong and of my error. I had never seen myself in such deformity as she saw me even when she used me with that divine compassion. I was almost glad to be what I was because of her angelic pity for me!"

The tears sprang to Don Ippolito's eyes, but Ferris asked in the same tone as before, "Was it then that she bade you be no longer a priest?"

"No, not then," patiently replied the other; "she was too greatly overwhelmed with my calamity to think of any cure for it. To-day it was that she uttered those words—words which I shall never forget, which will support and comfort me, whatever happens!"

The painter was biting hard upon the stem of his pipe. He turned away and began ordering the color-tubes and pencils on a table against the wall, putting them close together in very neat, straight rows. Presently he said: "Perhaps Miss Vervain also advised you to go to America?"

"Yes," answered the priest reverently. "She had thought of everything. She has promised me a refuge under her mother's roof there, until I can make my inventions known; and I shall follow them at once."

"Follow them?"

"They are going, she told me. Madama does not grow better. They are homesick. They—but you must know all this already?"

"Oh, not at all, not at all," said the painter with a very bitter smile. "You are telling me news. Pray go on."

"There is no more. She made me promise to come to you and listen to your advice before I took any step. I must not trust to her alone, she said; but if I took this step, then through whatever happened she would be my friend. Ah, dear friend, may I speak to you of the hope that these words gave me? You have seen—have you not?—you must have seen that"—The priest faltered, and Ferris stared at him helpless. When the next words came he could not find any strangeness in the fact which yet gave him so great a shock. He found that to his nether consciousness it had been long familiar—ever since that day when he had first jestingly proposed Don Ippolito as Miss Vervain's teacher. Grotesque, tragic, impossible—it had still been the under-current of all his reveries; or so now it seemed to have been.

Don Ippolito anxiously drew nearer to him and laid an imploring touch upon his arm,—"I love her!"

"What!" gasped the painter. "You? You I A priest?"

"Priest! priest!" cried Don Ippolito, violently. "From this day I am no longer a priest! From this hour I am a man, and I can offer her the honorable love of a man, the truth of a most sacred marriage, and fidelity to death!"

Ferris made no answer. He began to look very coldly and haughtily at Don Ippolito, whose heat died away under his stare, and who at last met it with a glance of tremulous perplexity. His hand had dropped from Ferris's arm, and he now moved some steps from him. "What is it, dear friend?" he besought him. "Is there something that offends you? I came to you for counsel, and you meet me with a repulse little short of enmity. I do not understand. Do I intend anything wrong without knowing it? Oh, I conjure you to speak plainly!"

"Wait! Wait a minute," said Ferris, waving his hand like a man tormented by a passing pain. "I am trying to think. What you say is.... I cannot imagine it!"

"Not imagine it? Not imagine it? And why? Is she not beautiful?"

"Yes."

"And good?"

"Without doubt."

"And young, and yet wise beyond her years? And true, and yet angelically kind?"

"It is all as you say, God knows. But.... a priest"—

"Oh! Always that accursed word! And at heart, what is a priest, then, but a man?—a wretched, masked, imprisoned, banished man! Has he not blood and nerves like you? Has he not eyes to see what is fair, and ears to hear what is sweet? Can he live near so divine a flower and not know her grace, not inhale the fragrance of her soul, not adore her beauty? Oh, great God! And if at last he would tear off his stifling mask, escape from his prison, return from his exile, would you gainsay him?"

"No!" said the painter with a kind of groan. He sat down in a tall, carven gothic chair,—the furniture of one of his pictures,—and rested his head against its high back and looked at the priest across the room. "Excuse me," he continued with a strong effort. "I am ready to befriend you to the utmost of my power. What was it you wanted to ask me? I have told you truly what I thought of your scheme of going to America; but I may very well be mistaken. Was it about that Miss Vervain desired you to consult me?" His voice and manner hardened again in spite of him. "Or did she wish me to advise you about the renunciation of your priesthood? You must have thought that carefully over for yourself."

"Yes, I do not think you could make me see that as a greater difficulty than it has appeared to me." He paused with a confused and daunted air, as if some important point had slipped his mind. "But I must take the step; the burden of the double part I play is unendurable, is it not?"

"You know better than I."

"But if you were such a man as I, with neither love for your vocation nor faith in it, should you not cease to be a priest?"

"If you ask me in that way,—yes," answered the painter. "But I advise you nothing. I could not counsel another in such a case."

"But you think and feel as I do," said the priest, "and I am right, then."

"I do not say you are wrong."

Ferris was silent while Don Ippolito moved up and down the room, with his sliding step, like some tall, gaunt, unhappy girl. Neither could put an end to this interview, so full of intangible, inconclusive misery. Ferris drew a long breath, and then said steadily, "Don Ippolito, I suppose you did not speak idly to me of your—your feeling for Miss Vervain, and that I may speak plainly to you in return."

"Surely," answered the priest, pausing in his walk and fixing his eyes upon the painter. "It was to you as the friend of both that I spoke of my love, and my hope—which is oftener my despair."

"Then you have not much reason to believe that she returns your— feeling?"

"Ah, how could she consciously return it? I have been hitherto a priest to her, and the thought of me would have been impurity. But hereafter, if I can prove myself a man, if I can win my place in the world.... No, even now, why should she care so much for my escape from these bonds, if she did not care for me more than she knew?"

"Have you ever thought of that extravagant generosity of Miss Vervain's character?"

"It is divine!"

"Has it seemed to you that if such a woman knew herself to have once wrongly given you pain, her atonement might be as headlong and excessive as her offense? That she could have no reserves in her reparation?"

Don Ippolito looked at Ferris, but did not interpose.

"Miss Vervain is very religious in her way, and she is truth itself. Are you sure that it is not concern for what seems to her your terrible position, that has made her show so much anxiety on your account?"

"Do I not know that well? Have I not felt the balm of her most heavenly pity?"

"And may she not be only trying to appeal to something in you as high as the impulse of her own heart?"

"As high!" cried Don Ippolito, almost angrily. "Can there be any higher thing in heaven or on earth than love for such a woman?"

"Yes; both in heaven and on earth," answered Ferris.

"I do not understand you," said Don Ippolito with a puzzled stare.

Ferris did not reply. He fell into a dull reverie in which he seemed to forget Don Ippolito and the whole affair. At last the priest spoke again: "Have you nothing to say to me, signore?"

"I? What is there to say?" returned the other blankly.

"Do you know any reason why I should not love her, save that I am—have been—a priest?"

"No, I know none," said the painter, wearily.

"Ah," exclaimed Don Ippolito, "there is something on your mind that you will not speak. I beseech you not to let me go wrong. I love her so well that I would rather die than let my love offend her. I am a man with the passions and hopes of a man, but without a man's experience, or a man's knowledge of what is just and right in these relations. If you can be my friend in this so far as to advise or warn me; if you can be her friend"—

Ferris abruptly rose and went to his balcony, and looked out upon the Grand Canal. The time-stained palace opposite had not changed in the last half-hour. As on many another summer day, he saw the black boats going by. A heavy, high-pointed barge from the Sile, with the captain's family at dinner in the shade of a matting on the roof, moved sluggishly down the middle current. A party of Americans in a gondola, with their opera-glasses and guide-books in their hands, pointed out to each other the eagle on the consular arms. They were all like sights in a mirror, or things in a world turned upside down.

Ferris came back and looked dizzily at the priest trying to believe that this unhuman, sacerdotal phantasm had been telling him that it loved a beautiful young girl of his own

W. D. Howells

race, faith, and language.

"Will you not answer me, signore?" meekly demanded Don
Ippolito.

"In this matter," replied the painter, "I cannot advise or warn
you. The whole affair is beyond my conception. I mean no
unkindness, but I cannot consult with you about it. There are
reasons why I should not. The mother of Miss Vervain is
here with her, and I do not feel that her interests in such a
matter are in my hands. If they come to me for help, that is
different. What do you wish? You tell me that you are
resolved to renounce the priesthood and go to America; and I
have answered you to the best of my power. You tell me that
you are in love with Miss Vervain. What can I have to say
about that?"

Don Ippolito stood listening with a patient, and then a
wounded air. "Nothing," he answered proudly. "I ask your
pardon for troubling you with my affairs. Your former
kindness emboldened me too much. I shall not trespass
again. It was my ignorance, which I pray you to excuse. I
take my leave, signore."

He bowed, and moved out of the room, and a dull remorse
filled the painter, as he heard the outer door close after him.
But he could do nothing. If he had given a wound to the
heart that trusted him, it was in an anguish which he had not
been able to master, and whose causes he could not yet
define. It was all a shapeless torment; it held him like the
memory of some hideous nightmare prolonging its horror
beyond sleep. It seemed impossible that what had happened
should have happened.

It was long, as he sat in the chair from which he had talked
with Don Ippolito, before he could reason about what had

been said; and then the worst phase presented itself first. He could not help seeing that the priest might have found cause for hope in the girl's behavior toward him. Her violent resentments, and her equally violent repentances; her fervent interest in his unhappy fortunes, and her anxiety that he should at once forsake the priesthood; her urging him to go to America, and her promising him a home under her mother's roof there: why might it not all be in fact a proof of her tenderness for him? She might have found it necessary to be thus coarsely explicit with him, for a man in Don Ippolito's relation to her could not otherwise have imagined her interest in him. But her making use of Ferris to confirm her own purposes by his words, her repeating them so that they should come back to him from Don Ippolito's lips, her letting another man go with her to look upon the procession in which her priestly lover was to appear in his sacerdotal panoply; these things could cot be accounted for except by that strain of insolent, passionate defiance which he had noted ill her from the beginning. Why should she first tell Don Ippolito of their going away? "Well, I wish him joy of his bargain," said Ferris aloud, and rising, shrugged his shoulders, and tried to cast off all care of a matter that did not concern him. But one does not so easily cast off a matter that does not concern one. He found himself haunted by certain tones and looks and attitudes of the young girl, wholly alien to the character he had just constructed for her. They were child-like, trusting, unconscious, far beyond anything he had yet known in women, and they appealed to him now with a maddening pathos. She was standing there before Don Ippolito's picture as on that morning when she came to Ferris, looking anxiously at him, her innocent beauty, troubled with some hidden care, hallowing the place. Ferris thought of the young fellow who told him that he had spent three months in a dull German town because he had the room there that was once occupied by the girl who had refused him; the painter remembered that the young fellow said he had just read of her marriage in an American newspaper.

Why did Miss Vervain send Don Ippolito to him? Was it some scheme of her secret love for the priest; or mere coarse resentment of the cautions Ferris had once hinted, a piece of vulgar bravado? But if she had acted throughout in pure simplicity, in unwise goodness of heart? If Don Ippolito were altogether self-deceived, and nothing but her unknowing pity had given him grounds of hope? He himself had suggested this to the priest, and how with a different motive he looked at it in his own behalf. A great load began slowly to lift itself from Ferris's heart, which could ache now for this most unhappy priest. But if his conjecture were just, his duty would be different. He must not coldly acquiesce and let things take their course. He had introduced Don Ippolito to the Vervains; he was in some sort responsible for him; he must save them if possible from the painful consequences of the priest's hallucination. But how to do this was by no means clear. He blamed himself for not having been franker with Don Ippolito and tried to make him see that the Vervains might regard his passion as a presumption upon their kindness to him, an abuse of their hospitable friendship; and yet how could he have done this without outrage to a sensitive and right-meaning soul? For a moment it seemed to him that he must seek Don Ippolito, and repair his fault; but they had hardly parted as friends, and his action might be easily misconstrued. If he shrank from the thought of speaking to him of the matter again, it appeared yet more impossible to bring it before the Vervains. Like a man of the imaginative temperament as he was, he exaggerated the probable effect, and pictured their dismay in colors that made his interference seem a ludicrous enormity; in fact, it would have been an awkward business enough for one not hampered by his intricate obligations. He felt bound to the Vervains, the ignorant young girl, and the addle-pated mother; but if he ought to go to them and tell them what he knew, to which of them ought he to speak, and how? In an anguish of perplexity that made the sweat stand in drops upon his forehead, he smiled to think it just possible that Mrs. Vervain might take the matter seriously, and wish to consider the propriety of Florida's accepting Don Ippolito. But if he spoke to the daughter, how should he approach the subject? "Don Ippolito tells me he loves you, and he goes to America with the expectation that when he has made his fortune with a patent back-action apple-corer, you will marry him." Should he say something to this purport? And in Heaven's name what right had he, Ferris, to say anything at all? The horrible absurdity, the inexorable delicacy of his position made him laugh.

On the other hand, besides, he was bound to Don Ippolito, who had come to him as the nearest friend of both, and confided in him. He remembered with a tardy, poignant intelligence how in their first talk of the Vervains Don Ippolito had taken pains to inform himself that Ferris was not in love with Florida. Could he be less manly and generous than this poor priest, and violate the sanctity of his confidence? Ferris groaned aloud. No, contrive it as he would, call it by what fair name he chose, he could not commit this treachery. It was the more impossible to him because, in this agony of doubt as to what he should do, he now at least read big own heart clearly, and had no longer a doubt what was in it. He pitied her for the pain she must suffer. He saw how her simple goodness, her blind sympathy with Don Ippolito, and only this, must have led the priest to the mistaken pass at which he stood. But Ferris felt that the whole affair had been fatally carried beyond his reach; he could do nothing now but wait and endure. There are cases in which a man must not protect the woman he loves. This was one.

The afternoon wore away. In the evening he went to the Piazza, and drank a cup of coffee at Florian's. Then he walked to the Public Gardens, where he watched the crowd till it thinned in the twilight and left him alone. He hung upon the parapet, looking off over the lagoon that at last he perceived to be flooded with moonlight. He desperately called a gondola, and bade the man row him to the public landing nearest the Vervains', and so walked up the calle, and entered the palace from the campo, through the court that on one side opened into the garden.

Mrs. Vervain was alone in the room where he had always been accustomed to find her daughter with her, and a chill as of the impending change fell upon him. He felt how pleasant it had been to find them together; with a vain, piercing regret he felt how much like home the place had been to him. Mrs. Vervain, indeed, was not changed; she was even more than ever herself, though all that she said imported change. She seemed to observe nothing unwonted in him, and she began to talk in her way of things that she could not know were so near his heart.

"Now, Mr. Ferris, I have a little surprise for you. Guess what it is!"

"I'm not good at guessing. I'd rather not know what it is than have to guess it," said Ferris, trying to be light, under his heavy trouble.

"You won't try once, even? Well, you're going to be rid of us soon I We are going away."

"Yes, I knew that," said Ferris quietly. "Don Ippolito told me so to-day."

"And is that all you have to say? Isn't it rather sad? Isn't it sudden? Come, Mr. Ferris, do be a little complimentary, for once!"

"It's sudden, and I can assure you it's sad enough for me," replied the painter, in a tone which could not leave any doubt of his sincerity.

"Well, so it is for us," quavered Mrs. Vervain. "You have been very, very good to us," she went on more collectedly, "and we shall never forget it. Florida has been speaking of it, too, and she's extremely grateful, and thinks we've quite imposed upon you."

"Thanks."

"I suppose we have, but as I always say, you're the representative of the country here. However, that's neither here nor there. We have no relatives on the face of the earth, you know; but I have a good many old friends in Providence, and we're going back there. We both think I shall be better at home; for I'm sorry to say, Mr. Ferns, that though I don't complain of Venice,—it's really a beautiful place, and all that; not the least exaggerated,—still I don't think it's done my health much good; or at least I don't seem to gain, don't you know, I don't seem to gain."

"I'm very sorry to hear it, Mrs. Vervain."

"Yes, I'm sure you are; but you see, don't you, that we must go? We are going next week. When we've once made up our minds, there's no object in prolonging the agony."

Mrs. Vervain adjusted her glasses with the thumb and finger of her right hand, and peered into Ferris's face with a gay smile. "But the greatest part of the surprise is," she resumed, lowering her voice a little, "that Don Ippolito is going with us."

"Ah!" cried Ferris sharply.

"I *knew* I should surprise you," laughed Mrs. Vervain. "We've been having a regular confab—*clave*, I mean—about it here, and he's all on fire to go to America; though it must be kept a great secret on his account, poor fellow. He's to join us in France, and then he can easily get into England, with us. You know he's to give up being a priest, and is going to devote himself to invention when ho gets to America. Now, what *do* you think of it, Mr. Ferris? Quite strikes you dumb, doesn't it?" triumphed Mrs. Vervain. "I suppose it's what you would call a wild goose chase,—I used to pick up all those phrases,— but we shall carry it through."

Ferris gasped, as though about to speak, but said nothing.

"Don Ippolito's been here the whole afternoon," continued Mrs. Vervain, "or rather ever since about five o'clock. He took dinner with us, and we've been talking it over and over. He's *so* enthusiastic about it, and yet he breaks down every little while, and seems quite to despair of the undertaking. But Florida won't let him do that; and really it's funny, the way he defers to her judgment—you know *I* always regard Florida as such a mere child—and seems to take every word she says for gospel. But, shedding tears, now: it's dreadful in a man, isn't it? I wish Don Ippolito wouldn't do that. It makes one creep. I can't feel that it's manly; can you?"

Ferris found voice to say something about those things being different with the Latin races.

"Well, at any rate," said Mrs. Vervain, "I'm glad that *Americans* don't shed tears, as a general *rule*. Now, Florida: you'd think she was the man all through this business, she's so perfectly heroic about it; that is, outwardly: for I can see—women can, in each other, Mr. Ferris—just where she's on the point of breaking down, all the while. Has she ever spoken to you about Don Ippolito? She does think so highly of your opinion, Mr. Ferris."

"She does me too much honor," said Ferris, with ghastly irony.

"Oh, I don't think so," returned Mrs. Vervain. "She told me this morning that she'd made Don Ippolito promise to speak to you about it; but he didn't mention having done so, and—I hated, don't you know, to ask him.... In fact, Florida had told me beforehand that I mustn't. She said he must be left entirely to himself in that matter, and"—Mrs. Vervain looked suggestively at Ferris.

"He spoke to me about it," said Ferris.

"Then why in the world did you let me run on? I suppose you advised him against it."

"I certainly did."

"Well, there's where I think woman's intuition is better than man's reason."

The painter silently bowed his head.

"Yes, I'm quite woman's rights in that respect," said Mrs. Vervain.

"Oh, without doubt," answered Ferris, aimlessly.

"I'm perfectly delighted," she went on, "at the idea of Don Ippolito's giving up the priesthood, and I've told him he must get married to some good American girl. You ought to have seen how the poor fellow blushed! But really, you know, there are lots of nice girls that would *jump* at him—so handsome and sad-looking, and a genius."

Ferris could only stare helplessly at Mrs. Vervain, who continued:—

"Yes, I think he's a genius, and I'm determined that he shall have a chance. I suppose we've got a job on our hands; but I'm not sorry. I'll introduce him into society, and if he needs money he shall have it. What does God give us money for, Mr. Ferris, but to help our fellow-creatures?"

So miserable, as he was, from head to foot, that it seemed impossible he could endure more, Ferris could not forbear laughing at this burst of piety.

"What are you laughing at?" asked Mrs. Vervain, who had cheerfully joined him. "Something I've been saying. Well, you won't have me to laugh at much longer. I do wonder whom you'll have next."

Ferris's merriment died away in something like a groan, and when Mrs. Vervain again spoke, it was in a tone of sudden querulousness. "I *wish* Florida would come! She went to bolt the land-gate after Don Ippolito,—I wanted her to,—but she ought to have been back long ago. It's odd you didn't meet them, coming in. She must be in the garden Somewhere; I suppose she's sorry to be leaving it. But I need her. Would you be so very kind, Mr. Ferris, as to go and ask her to come to me?"

Ferris rose heavily from the chair in which he seemed to have grown ten years older. He had hardly heard anything that he did not know already, but the clear vision of the affair with which he had come to the Vervains was hopelessly confused and darkened. He could make nothing of any phase of it. He did not know whether he cared now to see Florida or not. He mechanically obeyed Mrs. Vervain, and stepping out upon the terrace, slowly descended the stairway.

The moon was shining brightly into the garden.

W. D. Howells

XV

Florida and Don Ippolito had paused in the pathway which parted at the fountain and led in one direction to the water-gate, and in the other out through the palace-court into the campo.

"Now, you must not give way to despair again," she said to him. "You will succeed, I am sure, for you will deserve success."

"It is all your goodness, madamigella," sighed the priest, "and at the bottom of my heart I am afraid that all the hope and courage I have are also yours."

"You shall never want for hope and courage then. We believe in you, and we honor your purpose, and we will be your steadfast friends. But now you must think only of the present—of how you are to get away from Venice. Oh, I can understand how you must hate to leave it! What a beautiful night! You mustn't expect such moonlight as this in America, Don Ippolito."

"It *is* beautiful, is it not?" said the priest, kindling from her. "But I think we Venetians are never so conscious of the beauty of Venice as you strangers are."

"I don't know. I only know that now, since we tave made up our minds to go, and fixed the day and hour, it is more like leaving my own country than anything else I've ever felt. This garden, I seem to have spent my whole life in it; and when we are settled in Providence, I'm going to have mother send back for some of these statues. I suppose Signor Cavaletti wouldn't mind our robbing his place of them if he were paid enough. At any rate we must have this one that belongs to the fountain. You shall be the first to set the fountain playing over there, Don Ippolito, and then we'll sit down on this stone bench before it, and imagine ourselves in the garden of Casa Vervain at Venice."

"No, no; let me be the last to set it playing here," said the priest, quickly stooping to the pipe at the foot of the figure, "and then we will sit down here, and imagine ourselves in the garden of Casa Vervain at Providence."

Florida put her hand on his shoulder. "You mustn't do it," she said simply. "The padrone doesn't like to waste the water."

"Oh, we'll pray the saints to rain it back on him some day," cried Don Ippolito with willful levity, and the stream leaped into the moonlight and seemed to hang there like a tangled skein of silver. "But how shall I shut it off when you are gone?" asked the young girl, looking ruefully at the floating threads of splendor.

"Oh, I will shut it off before I go," answered Don Ippolito. "Let it play a moment," he continued, gazing rapturously upon it, while the moon painted his lifted face with a pallor that his black robes heightened. He fetched a long, sighing breath, as if he inhaled with that respiration all the rich odors of the flowers, blanched like his own visage in the white lustre; as if he absorbed into his heart at once the wide glory of the summer night, and the beauty of the young girl at his side. It seemed a supreme moment with him; he looked as a man might look who has climbed out of lifelong defeat into a single instant of release and triumph.

Florida sank upon the bench before the fountain, indulging his caprice with that sacred, motherly tolerance, some touch of which is in all womanly yielding to men's will, and which was perhaps present in greater degree in her feeling towards a man more than ordinarily orphaned and unfriended.

"Is Providence your native city?" asked Don Ippolito, abruptly, after a little silence.

"Oh no; I was born at St. Augustine in Florida."

"Ah yes, I forgot; madama has told me about it; Providence is *her* city. But the two are near together?"

"No," said Florida, compassionately, "they are a thousand miles apart."

"A thousand miles? What a vast country!"

"Yes, it's a whole world."

"Ah, a world, indeed!" cried the priest, softly. "I shall never comprehend it."

"You never will," answered the young girl gravely, "if you do not think about it more practically."

"Practically, practically!" lightly retorted the priest. "What a word with you Americans; That is the consul's word: *practical*."

"Then you have been to see him to-day?" asked Florida, with

eagerness. "I wanted to ask you"—

"Yes, I went to consult the oracle, as you bade me."

"Don Ippolito"—

"And he was averse to my going to America. He said it was not practical."

"Oh!" murmured the girl.

"I think," continued the priest with vehemence, "that Signor Ferris is no longer my friend."

"Did he treat you coldly—harshly?" she asked, with a note of indignation in her voice. "Did he know that I—that you came"—

"Perhaps he was right. Perhaps I shall indeed go to ruin there. Ruin, ruin! Do I not *live* ruin here?"

"What did he say—what did he tell you?"

"No, no; not now, madamigella! I do not want to think of that man, now. I want you to help me once more to realize myself in America, where I shall never have been a priest, where I shall at least battle even-handed with the world. Come, let us forget him; the thought of him palsies all my hope. He could not see me save in this robe, in this figure that I abhor."

"Oh, it was strange, it was not like him, it was cruel! What did he say?"

"In everything but words, he bade me despair; he bade me look upon all that makes life dear and noble as impossible to me!"

"Oh, how? Perhaps he did not understand you. No, he did not understand you. What did you say to him, Don Ippolito? Tell me!" She leaned towards him, in anxious emotion, as she spoke.

The priest rose, and stretched out his arms, as if he would gather something of courage from the infinite space. In his visage were the sublimity and the terror of a man who puts everything to the risk.

"How will it really be with me, yonder?" he demanded. "As it is with other men, whom their past life, if it has been guiltless, does not follow to that new world of freedom and justice?"

"Why should it not be so?" demanded Florida. "Did *he* say it would not?"

"Need it be known there that I have been a priest? Or if I tell it, will it make me appear a kind of monster, different from other men?"

"No, no!" she answered fervently. "Your story would gain friends and honor for you everywhere in America. Did *he*"—

"A moment, a moment!" cried Don Ippolito, catching his breath. "Will it ever be possible for me to win something more than honor and friendship there?"

She looked up at him askingly, confusedly.

"If I am a man, and the time should ever come that a face, a look, a voice, shall be to me what they are to other men, will *she* remember it against me that I have been a priest, when I tell her—say to her, madamigella—how dear she is to me, offer her my life's devotion, ask her to be my wife?"...

Florida rose from the seat, and stood confronting him, in a helpless silence, which he seemed not to notice.

Suddenly he clasped his hands together, and desperately stretched them towards her.

"Oh, my hope, my trust, my life, if it were you that I loved?"...

"What!" shuddered the girl, recoiling, with almost a shriek. "*You*? *A priest!*"

Don Ippolito gave a low cry, half sob:—

"His words, his words! It is true, I cannot escape, I am doomed, I must die as I have lived!"

He dropped his face into his hands, and stood with his head bowed before her; neither spoke for a long time, or moved.

Then Florida said absently, in the husky murmur to which her voice fell when she was strongly moved, "Yes, I see it all, how it has been," and was silent again, staring, as if a procession of the events and scenes of the past months were passing before her; and presently she moaned to herself "Oh, oh, oh!" and wrung her hands. The foolish fountain kept capering and babbling on. All at once, now, as a flame flashes up and then expires, it leaped and dropped extinct at the foot of the statue.

Its going out seemed somehow to leave them in darkness, and under cover of that gloom she drew nearer the priest, and by such approaches as one makes toward a fancied apparition, when his fear will not let him fly, but it seems better to suffer the worst from it at once than to live in terror of it ever after, she lifted her hands to his, and gently taking them away from his face, looked into his hopeless eyes.

"Oh, Don Ippolito," she grieved. "What shall I say to you, what can I do for you, now?"

But there was nothing to do. The whole edifice of his dreams, his wild imaginations, had fallen into dust at a word; no magic could rebuild it; the end that never seems the end had come. He let her keep his cold hands, and presently he returned the entreaty of her tears with his wan, patient smile.

"You cannot help me; there is no help for an error like mine. Sometime, if ever the thought of me is a greater pain than it is at this moment, you can forgive me. Yes, you can do that for me."

"But who, *who* will ever forgive me" she cried, "for my blindness! Oh, you must believe that I never thought, I never dreamt"—

"I know it well. It was your fatal truth that did it; truth too high and fine for me to have discerned save through such agony as.... You too loved my soul, like the rest, and you would have had me no priest for the reason that they would have had me a priest—I see it. But you had no right to love my soul and not me—you, a woman. A woman must not love only the soul of a man."

"Yes, yes!" piteously explained the girl, "but you were a priest to me!"

"That is true, madamigella. I was always a priest to you; and now I see that I never could be otherwise. Ah, the wrong began many years before we met. I was trying to blame you a little"—

"Blame me, blame me; do!"

—"but there is no blame. Think that it was another way of asking your forgiveness.... O my God, my God, my God!"

He released his hands from her, and uttered this cry under his breath, with his face lifted towards the heavens. When he looked at her again, he said: "Madamigella, if my share of this misery gives me the right to ask of you"—

"Oh ask anything of me! I will give everything, do everything!"

He faltered, and then, "You do not love me," he 8aid abruptly; "is there some one else that you love?"

She did not answer.

"Is it ... he?"

She hid her face.

"I knew it," groaned the priest, "I knew that too!" and he turned away.

"Don Ippolito, Don Ippolito—oh, poor, poor Don Ippolito!" cried the girl, springing towards him. "Is *this* the way you leave me? Where are you going? What will you do now?"

"Did I not say? I am going to die a priest."

"Is there nothing that you will let me be to you, hope for you?"

W. D. Howells

"Nothing," said Don Ippolito, after a moment. "What could you?" He seized the hands imploringly extended towards him, and clasped them together and kissed them both. "Adieu!" he whispered; then he opened them, and passionately kissed either palm; "adieu, adieu!"

A great wave of sorrow and compassion and despair for him swept through her. She flung her arms about his neck, and pulled his head down upon her heart, and held it tight there, weeping and moaning over him as over some hapless, harmless thing that she had unpurposely bruised or killed. Then she suddenly put her hands against his breast, and thrust him away, and turned and ran.

Ferris stepped back again into the shadow of the tree from which he had just emerged, and clung to its trunk lest he should fall. Another seemed to creep out of the court in his person, and totter across the white glare of the campo and down the blackness of the calle. In the intersected spaces where the moonlight fell, this alien, miserable man saw the figure of a priest gliding on before him.

XVI

Florida swiftly me anted the terrace steps, but she stopped with her hand on the door, panting, and turned and walked slowly away to the end of the terrace, drying her eyes with dashes of her handkerchief, and ordering her hair, some coils of which had been loosened by her flight. Then she went back to the door, waited, and softly opened it, Her mother was not in the parlor where she had left her, and she passed noiselessly into her own room, where some trunks stood open and half-packed against the wall. She began to gather up the pieces of dress that lay upon the bed and chairs, and to fold them with mechanical carefulness and put them in the boxes. Her mother's voice called from the other chamber, "Is that you, Florida?"

"Yes, mother," answered the girl, but remained kneeling before one of the boxes, with that pale green robe in her hand which she had worn on the morning when Ferris had first brought Don Ippolito to see them. She smoothed its folds and looked down at it without making any motion to pack it away, and so she lingered while her mother advanced with one question after another; "What are you doing, Florida? Where are you? Why didn't you come to me?" and finally stood in the doorway. "Oh, you're packing. Do you know, Florida, I'm getting very impatient about going. I wish we could be off at once."

A tremor passed over the young girl and she started from her languid posture, and laid the dress in the trunk. "So do I, mother. I would give the world if we could go to-morrow!"

"Yes, but we can't, you see. I'm afraid we've undertaken a great deal, my dear. It's quite a weight upon *my* mind, already; and I don't know what it *will* be. If we were free, now, I should say, go to-morrow, by all means. But we couldn't arrange it with Don Ippolito on our hands."

Florida waited a moment before she replied. Then she said coldly, "Don Ippolito is not going with us, mother."

"Not going with us? Why"—

"He is not going to America. He will not leave Venice; he is to remain a priest," said Florida, doggedly.

Mrs. Vervain sat down in the chair that stood beside the door. "Not going to America; not leave Venice; remain a priest? Florida, you astonish me! But I am not the least surprised, not the least in the world. I thought Don Ippolito would give out, all along. He is not what I should call fickle, exactly, but he is weak, or timid, rather. He is a good man, but he lacks courage, resolution. I always doubted if he would succeed in America; he is too much of a dreamer. But this, really, goes a little beyond anything. I never expected this. What did he say, Florida? How did he excuse himself?"

"I hardly know; very little. What was there to say?"

"To be sure, to be sure. Did you try to reason with him, Florida?"

"No," answered the girl, drearily.

"I am glad of that. I think you had said quite enough already. You owed it to yourself not to do so, and he might have misinterpreted it. These foreigners are very different from Americans. No doubt we should have had a time of it, if he had gone with us. It must be for the best. I'm sure it was ordered so. But all that doesn't relieve Don Ippolito from the charge of black ingratitude, and want of consideration for us. He's quite made fools of us."

"He was not to blame. It was a very great step for him. And if"....

"I know that. But he ought not to have talked of it. He ought to have known his own mind fully before speaking; that's the only safe way. Well, then, there is nothing to prevent our going to-morrow."

Florida drew a long breath, and rose to go on with the work of packing.

"Have you been crying, Florida? Well, of course, you can't help feeling sorry for such a man. There's a great deal of good in Don Ippolito, a great deal. But when you come to my age you won't cry so easily, my dear. It's very trying," said Mrs. Vervain. She sat awhile in silence before she asked: "Will he come here to-morrow morning?"

Her daughter looked at her with a glance of terrified inquiry.

"Do have your wits about you, my dear! We can't go away without saying good-by to him, and we can't go away without paying him."

"Paying him?"

"Yes, paying him—paying him for your lessons. It's always

been very awkward. He hasn't been like other teachers, you know: more like a guest, or friend of the family. He never seemed to want to take the money, and of late, I've been letting it run along, because I hated so to offer it, till now, it's quite a sum. I suppose he needs it, poor fellow. And how to get it to him is the question. He may not come to-morrow, as usual, and I couldn't trust it to the padrone. We might send it to him in a draft from Paris, but I'd rather pay him before we go. Besides, it would be rather rude, going away without seeing him again." Mrs. Vervain thought a moment; then, "I'll tell you," she resumed. "If he doesn't happen to come here to-morrow morning, we can stop on our way to the station and give him the money."

Florida did not answer.

"Don't you think that would be a good plan?"

"I don't know," replied the girl in a dull way.

"Why, Florida, if you think from anything Don Ippolito said that he would rather not see us again—that it would be painful to him—why, we could ask Mr. Ferris to hand him the money."

"Oh no, no, no, mother!" cried Florida, hiding her face, "that would be too horribly indelicate!"

"Well, perhaps it wouldn't be quite good taste," said Mrs. Vervain perturbedly, "but you needn't express yourself so violently, my dear. It's not a matter of life and death. I'm sure I don't know what to do. We must stop at Don Ippolito's house, I suppose. Don't you think so?"

"Yes," faintly assented the daughter.

Mrs. Vervain yawned. "Well I can't think anything more about it to-night; I'm too stupid. But that's the way we shall do. Will you help me to bed, my dear? I shall be good for nothing to-morrow."

She went on talking of Don Ippolito's change of purpose till her head touched the pillow, from which she suddenly lifted it again, and called out to her daughter, who had passed into the next room: "But Mr. Ferris—why didn't he come back with you?"

"Come back with me?"

"Why yes, child. I sent him out to call you, just before you came in. This Don Ippolito business put him quite out of my head. Didn't you see him? ... Oh! What's that?"

"Nothing: I dropped my candle."

"You're sure you didn't set anything on fire?"

"No! It went dead out."

"Light it again, and do look. Now is everything right?"

"Yes."

"It's queer he didn't come back to *say* he couldn't find you. What do you suppose became of him?"

"I don't know, mother."

"It's very perplexing. I wish Mr. Ferris were not so odd. It quite borders on affectation. I don't know what to make of it. We must send word to him the very first thing to-morrow morning, that we're going, and ask him to come to see us."

Florida made no reply. She sat staring at the black space of the door-way into her mother's room. Mrs. Vervain did not speak again. After a while her daughter softly entered her chamber, shading the candle with her hand; and seeing that she slept, softly withdrew, closed the door, and went about the work of packing again. When it was all done, she flung herself upon her bed and hid her face in the pillow.

* * * * *

The next morning was spent in bestowing those interminable last touches which the packing of ladies' baggage demands, and in taking leave with largess (in which Mrs. Vervain shone) of all the people in the house and out of it, who had so much as touched a hat to the Vervains during their sojourn. The whole was not a vast sum; nor did the sundry extortions of the padrone come to much, though the honest man racked his brain to invent injuries to his apartments and furniture. Being unmurmuringly paid, he gave way to his real goodwill for his tenants in many little useful offices. At the end he persisted in sending them to the station in his own gondola and could with difficulty be kept from going with them.

Mrs. Vervain had early sent a message to Ferris, but word came back a first and a second time that he was not at home, and the forenoon wore away and he had not appeared. A certain indignation sustained her till the gondola pushed out into the canal, and then it yielded to an intolerable regret that she should not see him.

"I *can't* go without saying good-by to Mr. Ferris, Florida," she said at last, "and it's no use asking me. He may have been wanting a little in politeness, but he's been *so* good all along; and we owe him too much not to make an effort to thank him before we go. We really must stop a moment at his house."

Florida, who had regarded her mother's efforts to summon Ferris to them with passive coldness, turned a look of agony upon her. But in a moment she bade the gondolier stop at the consulate, and dropping her veil over her face, fell back in the shadow of the tenda-curtains.

Mrs. Vervain sentimentalized their departure a little, but her daughter made no comment on the scene they were leaving.

The gondolier rang at Ferris's door and returned with the answer that he was not at home.

Mrs. Vervain gave way to despair. "Oh dear, oh dear! This is too bad! What shall we do?"

"We'll lose the train, mother, if we loiter in this way," said Florida.

"Well, wait. I *must* leave a message at least." "*How could you be away*," she wrote on her card, "*when we called to say good-by? We've changed our plans and we're going to-day. I shall write you a nice scolding letter from Verona—we're going over the Brenner—for your behavior last night. Who will keep you straight when I'm gone? You've been very, very kind. Florida joins me in a thousand thanks, regrets, and good-byes.*"

"There, I haven't said anything, after all," she fretted, with tears in her eyes.

The gondolier carried the card again to the door, where Ferris's servant let down a basket by a string and fished it up.

"If Don Ippolito shouldn't be in," said Mrs. Vervain, as the

W. D. Howells

boat moved on again, "I don't know what I *shall* do with this money. It will be awkward beyond anything."

The gondola slipped from the Canalazzo into the network of the smaller canals, where the dense shadows were as old as the palaces that cast them and stopped at the landing of a narrow quay. The gondolier dismounted and rang at Don Ippolito's door. There was no response; he rang again and again. At last from a window of the uppermost story the head of the priest himself peered out. The gondolier touched his hat and said, "It is the ladies who ask for you, Don Ippolito."

It was a minute before the door opened, and the priest, bare-headed and blinking in the strong light, came with a stupefied air across the quay to the landing-steps.

"Well, Don Ippolito!" cried Mrs. Vervain, rising and giving him her hand, which she first waved at the trunks and bags piled up in the vacant space in the front of the boat, "what do you think of this? We are really going, immediately; *we* can change our minds too; and I don't think it would have been too much," she added with a friendly smile, "if we had gone without saying good-by to you. What in the world does it all mean, your giving up that grand project of yours so suddenly?"

She sat down again, that she might talk more at her ease, and seemed thoroughly happy to have Don Ippolito before her again.

"It finally appeared best, madama," he said quietly, after a quick, keen glance at Florida, who did not lift her veil.

"Well, perhaps you're partly right. But I can't help thinking that you with your talent would have succeeded in America. Inventors do get on there, in the most surprising way. There's the Screw Company of Providence. It's such a simple thing; and now the shares are worth eight hundred. Are you well to-day, Don Ippolito?"

"Quite well, madama."

"I thought you looked rather pale. But I believe you're always a little pale. You mustn't work too hard. We shall miss you a great deal, Don Ippolito."

"Thanks, madama."

"Yes, we shall be quite lost without you. And I wanted to say this to you, Don Ippolito, that if ever you change your mind again, and conclude to come to America, you must write to me, and let me help you just as I had intended to do."

The priest shivered, as if cold, and gave another look at Florida's veiled face.

"You are too good," he said.

"Yes, I really think I am," replied Mrs. Vervain, playfully. "Considering that you were going to let me leave Venice without even trying to say good-by to me, I think I'm very good indeed."

Mrs. Vervain's mood became overcast, and her eyes filled with tears: "I hope you're sorry to have us going, Don Ippolito, for you know how very highly I prize your acquaintance. It was rather cruel of you, I think."

She seemed not to remember that he could not have known of their change of plan. Don Ippolito looked imploringly into her face, and made a touching gesture of deprecation, but did not speak.

W. D. Howells

"I'm really afraid you're *not* well, and I think it's too bad of us to be going," resumed Mrs. Vervain; "but it can't be helped now: we are all packed, don't you see. But I want to ask one favor of you, Don Ippolito; and that is," said Mrs. Vervain, covertly taking a little *rouleau* from her pocket, "that you'll leave these inventions of yours for a while, and give yourself a vacation. You need rest of mind. Go into the country, somewhere, do. That's what's preying upon you. But we must really be off, now. Shake hands with Florida—I'm going to be the last to part with you," she said, with a tearful smile.

Don Ippolito and Florida extended their hands. Neither spoke, and as she sank back upon the seat from which she had half risen, she drew more closely the folds of the veil which she had not lifted from her face.

Mrs. Vervain gave a little sob as Don Ippolito took her hand and kissed it; and she had some difficulty in leaving with him the rouleau, which she tried artfully to press into his palm. "Good-by, good-by," she said, "don't drop it," and attempted to close his fingers over it.

But he let it lie carelessly in his open hand, as the gondola moved off, and there it still lay as he stood watching the boat slip under a bridge at the next corner, and disappear. While he stood there gazing at the empty arch, a man of a wild and savage aspect approached. It was said that this man's brain had been turned by the death of his brother, who was betrayed to the Austrians after the revolution of '48, by his wife's confessor. He advanced with swift strides, and at the moment he reached Don Ippolito's side he suddenly turned his face upon him and cursed him through his clenched teeth: "Dog of a priest!"

Don Ippolito, as if his whole race had renounced him in the

maniac's words, uttered a desolate cry, and hiding his face in his hands, tottered into his house.

The rouleau had dropped from his palm; it rolled down the shelving marble of the quay, and slipped into the water.

The young beggar who had held Mrs. Vervain's gondola to the shore while she talked, looked up and down the deserted quay, and at the doors and windows. Then he began to take off his clothes for a bath.

XVII

Ferris returned at nightfall to his house, where he had not been since daybreak, and flung himself exhausted upon the bed. His face was burnt red with the sun, and his eyes were bloodshot. He fell into a doze and dreamed that he was still at Malamocco, whither he had gone that morning in a sort of craze, with some fishermen, who were to cast their nets there; then he was rowing back to Venice across the lagoon, that seemed a molten fire under the keel. He woke with a heavy groan, and bade Marina fetch him a light.

She set it on the table, and handed him the card Mrs. Vervain had left. He read it and read it again, and then he laid it down, and putting on his hat, he took his cane and went out. "Do not Wait for me, Marina," he said, "I may be late. Go to bed."

He returned at midnight, and lighting his candle took up the card and read it once more. He could not tell whether to be glad or sorry that he had failed to see the Vervains again. He took it for granted that Don Ippolito was to follow; he would not ask himself what motive had hastened their going. The reasons were all that he should never more look upon the woman so hatefully lost to him, but a strong instinct of his heart struggled against them.

He lay down in his clothes, and began to dream almost before he began to sleep. He woke early, and went out to walk. He did not rest all day. Once he came home, and found a letter from Mrs. Vervain, postmarked Verona, reiterating her lamentations and adieux, and explaining that the priest had relinquished his purpose, and would not go to America at all. The deeper mystery in which this news left him was not less sinister than before.

In the weeks that followed, Ferris had no other purpose than to reduce the days to hours, the hours to minutes. The burden that fell upon him when he woke lay heavy on his heart till night, and oppressed him far into his sleep. He could not give his trouble certain shape; what was mostly with him was a formless loss, which he could not resolve into any definite shame or wrong. At times, what he had seen seemed to him some baleful trick of the imagination, some lurid and foolish illusion.

But he could do nothing, he could not ask himself what the end was to be. He kept indoors by day, trying to work, trying to read, marveling somewhat that he did not fall sick and die. At night he set out on long walks, which took him he cared not where, and often detained him till the gray lights of morning began to tremble through the nocturnal blue. But even by night he shunned the neighborhood in which the Vervains had lived. Their landlord sent him a package of trifles they had left behind, but he refused to receive them, sending back word that he did not know where the ladies were. He had half expected that Mrs. Vervain, though he had not answered her last letter, might write to him again from England, but she did not. The Vervains had passed out of his world; he knew that they had been in it only by the torment they had left him.

He wondered in a listless way that he should see nothing of

W. D. Howells

Don Ippolito. Once at midnight he fancied that the priest was coming towards him across a campo he had just entered; he stopped and turned back into the calle: when the priest came up to him, it was not Don Ippolito.

In these days Ferris received a dispatch from the Department of State, informing him that his successor had been appointed, and directing him to deliver up the consular flags, seals, archives, and other property of the United States. No reason for his removal was given; but as there had never been any reason for his appointment, he had no right to complain; the balance was exactly dressed by this simple device of our civil service. He determined not to wait for the coming of his successor before giving up the consular effects, and he placed them at once in the keeping of the worthy ship-chandler who had so often transferred them from departing to arriving consuls. Then being quite ready at any moment to leave Venice, he found himself in nowise eager to go; but he began in a desultory way to pack up his sketches and studies.

One morning as he sat idle in his dismantled studio, Marina came to tell him that an old woman, waiting at the door below, wished to speak with him.

"Well, let her come up," said Ferris wearily, and presently Marina returned with a very ill-favored beldam, who stared hard at him while he frowningly puzzled himself as to where he had seen that malign visage before.

"Well?" he said harshly.

"I come," answered the old woman, "on the part of Don Ippolito Rondinelli, who desires so much to see your excellency."

Ferris made no response, while the old woman knotted the fringe of her shawl with quaking hands, and presently added with a tenderness in her voice which oddly discorded with the hardness of her face: "He has been very sick, poor thing, with a fever; but now he is in his senses again, and the doctors say he will get well. I hope so. But he is still very weak. He tried to write two lines to you, but he had not the strength; so he bade me bring you this word: That he had something to say which it greatly concerned you to hear, and that he prayed you to forgive his not coming to revere you, for it was impossible, and that you should have the goodness to do him this favor, to come to find him the quickest you could."

The old woman wiped her eyes with the corner of her shawl, and her chin wobbled pathetically while she shot a glance of baleful dislike at Ferris, who answered after a long dull stare at her, "Tell him I'll come."

He did not believe that Don Ippolito could tell him anything that greatly concerned him; but he was worn out with going round in the same circle of conjecture, and so far as he could be glad, he was glad of this chance to face his calamity. He would go, but not at once; he would think it over; he would go to-morrow, when he had got some grasp of the matter.

The old woman lingered.

"Tell him I'll come," repeated Ferris impatiently.

"A thousand excuses; but my poor master has been very sick. The doctors say he will get well. I hope so. But he is very weak indeed; a little shock, a little disappointment.... Is the signore very, *very* much occupied this morning? He greatly desired,—he prayed that if such a thing were possible in the goodness of your excellency .... But I am offending the signore!"

"What do you want?" demanded Ferris.

The old wretch set up a pitiful whimper, and tried to possess herself of his hand; she kissed his coat-sleeve instead. "That you will return with me," she besought him.

"Oh, I'll go!" groaned the painter. "I might as well go first as last," he added in English. "There, stop that! Enough, enough, I tell you! Didn't I say I was going with you?" he cried to the old woman.

"God bless you!" she mumbled, and set off before him down the stairs and out of the door. She looked so miserably old and weary that he called a gondola to his landing and made her get into it with him.

It tormented Don Ippolito's idle neighborhood to see Veneranda arrive in such state, and a passionate excitement arose at the caffe, where the person of the consul was known, when Ferris entered the priest's house with her.

He had not often visited Don Ippolito, but the quaintness of the place had been so vividly impressed upon him, that he had a certain familiarity with the grape-arbor of the ante-room, the paintings of the parlor, and the puerile arrange-ment of the piano and melodeon. Veneranda led him through these rooms to the chamber where Don Ippolito had first shown him his inventions. They were all removed now, and on a bed, set against the wall opposite the door, lay the priest, with his hands on his breast, and a faint smile on his lips, so peaceful, so serene, that the painter stopped with a sudden awe, as if he had unawares come into the presence of death.

"Advance, advance," whispered the old woman.

Near the head of the bed sat a white-haired priest wearing the red stockings of a canonico; his face was fanatically stern; but he rose, and bowed courteously to Ferris.

The stir of his robes roused Don Ippolito. He slowly and weakly turned his head, and his eyes fell upon the painter. He made a helpless gesture of salutation with his thin hand, and began to excuse himself, for the trouble he had given, with a gentle politeness that touched the painter's heart through all the complex resentments that divided them. It was indeed a strange ground on which the two men met. Ferris could not have described Don Ippolito as his enemy, for the priest had wittingly done him no wrong; he could not have logically hated him as a rival, for till it was too late he had not confessed to his own heart the love that was in it; he knew no evil of Don Ippolito, he could not accuse him of any betrayal of trust, or violation of confidence. He felt merely that this hapless creature, lying so deathlike before him, had profaned, however involuntarily, what was sacredest in the world to him; beyond this all was chaos. He had heard of the priest's sickness with a fierce hardening of the heart; yet as he beheld him now, he began to remember things that moved him to a sort of remorse. He recalled again the simple loyalty with which Don Ippolito had first spoken to him of Miss Vervain and tried to learn his own feeling toward her; he thought how trustfully at their last meeting the priest had declared his love and hope, and how, when he had coldly received his confession, Don Ippolito had solemnly adjured him to be frank with him; and Ferris could not. That pity for himself as the prey of fantastically cruel chances, which he had already vaguely felt, began now also to include the priest; ignoring all but that compassion, he went up to the bed and took the weak, chill, nerveless hand in his own.

The canonico rose and placed his chair for Ferris beside the pillow, on which lay a brass crucifix, and then softly left the room, exchanging a glance of affectionate intelligence with the sick man.

"I might have waited a little while," said Don Ippolito weakly, speaking in a hollow voice that was the shadow of his old deep tones, "but you will know how to forgive the impatience of a man not yet quite master of himself. I thank you for coming. I have been very sick, as you see; I did not think to live; I did not care.... I am very weak, now; let me say to you quickly what I want to say. Dear friend," continued Don Ippolito, fixing his eyes upon the painter's face, "I spoke to her that night after I had parted from you."

The priest's voice was now firm; the painter turned his face away.

"I spoke without hope," proceeded Don Ippolito, "and because I must. I spoke in vain; all was lost, all was past in a moment."

The coil of suspicions and misgivings and fears in which Ferris had lived was suddenly without a clew; he could not look upon the pallid visage of the priest lest he should now at last find there that subtle expression of deceit; the whirl of his thoughts kept him silent; Don Ippolito went on.

"Even if I had never been a priest, I would still have been impossible to her. She"....

He stopped as if for want of strength to go on. All at once he cried, "Listen!" and he rapidly recounted the story of his life, ending with the fatal tragedy of his love. When it was told, he said calmly, "But now everything is over with me on earth. I thank the Infinite Compassion for the sorrows through which I have passed. I, also, have proved the miraculous power of the church, potent to save in all ages." He gathered the crucifix in his spectral grasp, and pressed it to his lips. "Many merciful things have befallen me on this bed of sickness. My uncle, whom the long years of my darkness divided from me, is once more at peace with me. Even that poor old woman whom I sent to call you, and who had served me as I believed with hate for me as a false priest in her heart, has devoted herself day and night to my helplessness; she has grown decrepit with her cares and vigils. Yes, I have had many and signal marks of the divine pity to be grateful for." He paused, breathing quickly, and then added, "They tell me that the danger of this sickness is past. But none the less I have died in it. When I rise from this bed it shall be to take the vows of a Carmelite friar."

Ferris made no answer, and Don Ippolito resumed:—

"I have told you how when I first owned to her the falsehood in which I lived, she besought me to try if I might not find consolation in the holy life to which I had been devoted. When you see her, dear friend, will you not tell her that I came to understand that this comfort, this refuge, awaited me in the cell of the Carmelite? I have brought so much trouble into her life that I would fain have her know I have found peace where she bade me seek it, that I have mastered my affliction by reconciling myself to it. Tell her that but for her pity and fear for me, I believe that I must have died in my sins."

It was perhaps inevitable from Ferris's Protestant association of monks and convents and penances chiefly with the machinery of fiction, that all this affected him as unreally as talk in a stage-play. His heart was cold, as he answered: "I am glad that your mind is at rest concerning the doubts which so long troubled you. Not all men are so easily pacified; but, as you say, it is the privilege of your church to work miracles. As to Miss Vervain, I am sorry that I cannot promise to give her your message. I shall never see her again. Excuse me," he continued, "but your servant said there was something you wished to say that concerned me?"

"You will never see her again!" cried the priest, struggling to lift himself upon his elbow and falling back upon the pillow. "Oh, bereft! Oh, deaf and blind! It was *you* that she loved! She confessed it to me that night."

"Wait!" said Ferris, trying to steady his voice, and failing; "I was with Mrs. Vervain that night; she sent me into the garden to call her daughter, and I saw how Miss Vervain parted from the man she did not love! I saw".…

It was a horrible thing to have said it, he felt now that he had spoken; a sense of the indelicacy, the shamefulness, seemed to alienate him from all high concern in the matter, and to leave him a mere self-convicted eavesdropper. His face flamed; the wavering hopes, the wavering doubts alike died in his heart. He had fallen below the dignity of his own trouble.

"You saw, you saw," softly repeated the priest, without looking at him, and without any show of emotion; apparently, the convalescence that had brought him perfect clearness of reason had left his sensibilities still somewhat dulled. He closed his lips and lay silent. At last, he asked very gently, "And how shall I make you believe that what you saw was not a woman's love, but an angel's heavenly pity for me? Does it seem hard to believe this of her?"

"Yes," answered the painter doggedly, "it is hard."

"And yet it is the very truth. Oh, you do not know her, you

never knew her! In the same moment that she denied me her love, she divined the anguish of my soul, and with that embrace she sought to console me for the friendlessness of a whole life, past and to come. But I know that I waste my words on you," he cried bitterly. "You never would see me as I was; you would find no singleness in me, and yet I had a heart as full of loyalty to you as love for her. In what have I been false to you?"

"You never were false to me," answered Ferris, "and God knows I have been true to you, and at what cost. We might well curse the day we met, Don Ippolito, for we have only done each other harm. But I never meant you harm. And now I ask you to forgive me if I cannot believe you. I cannot— yet. I am of another race from you, slow to suspect, slow to trust. Give me a little time; let me see you again. I want to go away and think. I don't question your truth. I'm afraid you don't know. I'm afraid that the same deceit has tricked us both. I must come to you to-morrow. Can I?"

He rose and stood beside the couch.

"Surely, surely," answered the priest, looking into Ferris's troubled eyes with calm meekness. "You will do me the greatest pleasure. Yes, come again to-morrow. You know," he said with a sad smile, referring to his purpose of taking vows, "that my time in the world is short. Adieu, to meet again!"

He took Ferris's hand, hanging weak and hot by his side, and drew him gently down by it, and kissed him on either bearded cheek. "It is our custom, you know, among *friends*. Farewell."

The canonico in the anteroom bowed austerely to him as he passed through; the old woman refused with a harsh

W. D. Howells

"Nothing!" the money he offered her at the door.

He bitterly upbraided himself for the doubts he could not banish, and he still flushed with shame that he should have declared his knowledge of a scene which ought, at its worst, to have been inviolable by his speech. He scarcely cared now for the woman about whom these miseries grouped themselves; he realized that a fantastic remorse may be stronger than a jealous love.

He longed for the morrow to come, that he might confess his shame and regret; but a reaction to this violent repentance came before the night fell. As the sound of the priest's voice and the sight of his wasted face faded from the painter's sense, he began to see everything in the old light again. Then what Don Ippolito had said took a character of ludicrous, of insolent improbability.

After dark, Ferris set out upon one of his long, rambling walks. He walked hard and fast, to try if he might not still, by mere fatigue of body, the anguish that filled his soul. But whichever way he went he came again and again to the house of Don Ippolito, and at last he stopped there, leaning against the parapet of the quay, and staring at the house, as though he would spell from the senseless stones the truth of the secret they sheltered. Far up in the chamber, where he knew that the priest lay, the windows were dimly lit.

As he stood thus, with his upturned face haggard in the moonlight, the soldier commanding the Austrian patrol which passed that way halted his squad, and seemed about to ask him what he wanted there.

Ferris turned and walked swiftly homeward; but he did not even lie down. His misery took the shape of an intent that would not suffer him to rest. He meant to go to Don Ippolito and tell him that his story had failed of its effect, that he was not to be fooled so easily, and, without demanding anything further, to leave him in his lie.

At the earliest hour when he might hope to be admitted, he went, and rang the bell furiously. The door opened, and he confronted the priest's servant. "I want to see Don Ippolito," said Ferris abruptly.

"It cannot be," she began.

"I tell you I must," cried Ferris, raising his voice. "I tell you."....

"Madman!" fiercely whispered the old woman, shaking both her open hands in his face, "he's dead! He died last night!"

XVIII

The terrible stroke sobered Ferris, he woke from his long debauch of hate and jealousy and despair; for the first time since that night in the garden, he faced his fate with a clear mind. Death had set his seal forever to a testimony which he had been able neither to refuse nor to accept; in abject sorrow and shame he thanked God that he had been kept from dealing that last cruel blow; but if Don Ippolito had come back from the dead to repeat his witness, Ferris felt that the miracle could not change his own passive state. There was now but one thing in the world for him to do: to see Florida, to confront her with his knowledge of all that had been, and to abide by her word, whatever it was. At the worst, there was the war, whose drums had already called to him, for a refuge.

He thought at first that he might perhaps overtake the Vervains before they sailed for America, but he remembered that they had left Venice six weeks before. It seemed impossible that he could wait, but when he landed in New York, he was tormented in his impatience by a strange reluctance and hesitation. A fantastic light fell upon his plans; a sense of its wildness enfeebled his purpose. What was he going to do? Had he come four thousand miles to tell Florida that Don Ippolito was dead? Or was he going to say, "I have heard that you love me, but I don't believe it: is it true?"

He pushed on to Providence, stifling these antic misgivings as he might, and without allowing himself time to falter from his intent, he set out to find Mrs. Vervain's house. He knew the street and the number, for she had often given him the address in her invitations against the time when he should return to America. As he drew near the house a tender trepidation filled him and silenced all other senses in him; his heart beat thickly; the universe included only the fact that he was to look upon the face he loved, and this fact had neither past nor future.

But a terrible foreboding as of death seized him when he stood before the house, and glanced up at its close-shuttered front, and round upon the dusty grass-plots and neglected flower-beds of the door-yard. With a cold hand he rang and rang again, and no answer came. At last a man lounged up to the fence from the next house-door. "Guess you won't make anybody hear," he said, casually.

"Doesn't Mrs. Vervain live in this house?" asked Ferris, finding a husky voice in his throat that sounded to him like some other's voice lost there.

"She used to, but she isn't at home. Family's in Europe."

They had not come back yet.

"Thanks," said Ferris mechanically, and he went away. He laughed to himself at this keen irony of fortune; he was prepared for the confirmation of his doubts; he was ready for relief from them, Heaven knew; but this blank that the turn of the wheel had brought, this Nothing!

The Vervains were as lost to him as if Europe were in

another planet. How should he find them there? Besides, he was poor; he had no money to get back with, if he had wanted to return.

He took the first train to New York, and hunted up a young fellow of his acquaintance, who in the days of peace had been one of the governor's aides. He was still holding this place, and was an ardent recruiter. He hailed with rapture the expression of Ferris's wish to go into the war. "Look here!" he said after a moment's thought, "didn't you have some rank as a consul?"

"Yes," replied Ferris with a dreary smile, "I have been equivalent to a commander in the navy and a colonel in the army—I don't mean both, but either."

"Good!" cried his friend. "We must strike high. The colonelcies are rather inaccessible, just at present, and so are the lieutenant-colonelcies, but a majorship, now"....

"Oh no; don't!" pleaded Ferris. "Make me a corporal—or a cook. I shall not be so mischievous to our own side, then, and when the other fellows shoot me, I shall not be so much of a loss."

"Oh, they won't *shoot* you," expostulated his friend, high-heartedly. He got Ferris a commission as second lieutenant, and lent him money to buy a uniform.

Ferris's regiment was sent to a part of the southwest, where he saw a good deal of fighting and fever and ague. At the end of two years, spent alternately in the field and the hospital, he was riding out near the camp one morning in unusual spirits, when two men in butternut fired at him: one had the mortification to miss him; the bullet of the other struck him in the arm. There was talk of amputation at first, but the case was finally managed without. In Ferris's state of health it was quite the same an end of his soldiering.

He came North sick and maimed and poor. He smiled now to think of confronting Florida in any imperative or challenging spirit; but the current of his hopeless melancholy turned more and more towards her. He had once, at a desperate venture, written to her at Providence, but he had got no answer. He asked of a Providence man among the artists in New York, if he knew the Vervains; the Providence man said that he did know them a little when he was much younger; they had been abroad a great deal; he believed in a dim way that they were still in Europe. The young one, he added, used to have a temper of her own.

"Indeed!" said Ferris stiffly.

The one fast friend whom he found in New York was the governor's dashing aide. The enthusiasm of this recruiter of regiments had not ceased with Ferris's departure for the front; the number of disabled officers forbade him to lionize any one of them, but he befriended Ferris; he made a feint of discovering the open secret of his poverty, and asked how he could help him.

"I don't know," said Ferris, "it looks like a hopeless case, to me."

"Oh no it isn't," retorted his friend, as cheerfully and confidently as he had promised him that he should not be shot. "Didn't you bring back any pictures from Venice with you?"

"I brought back a lot of sketches and studies. I'm sorry to say that I loafed a good deal there; I used to feel that I had eternity before me; and I was a theorist and a purist and an idiot generally. There are none of them fit to be seen."

"Never mind; let's look at them."

They hunted out Ferris's property from a catch-all closet in the studio of a sculptor with whom he had left them, and who expressed a polite pleasure in handing them over to Ferris rather than to his heirs and assigns.

"Well, I'm not sure that I share your satisfaction, old fellow," said the painter ruefully; but he unpacked the sketches.

Their inspection certainly revealed a disheartening condition of half-work. "And I can't do anything to help the matter for the present," groaned Ferris, stopping midway in the business, and making as if to shut the case again.

"Hold on," said his friend. "What's this? Why, this isn't so bad." It was the study of Don Ippolito as a Venetian priest, which Ferris beheld with a stupid amaze, remembering that he had meant to destroy it, and wondering how it had got where it was, but not really caring much. "It's worse than you can imagine," said he, still looking at it with this apathy.

"No matter; I want you to sell it to me. Come!"

"I can't!" replied Ferris piteously. "It would be flat burglary."

"Then put it into the exhibition."

The sculptor, who had gone back to scraping the chin of the famous public man on whose bust he was at work, stabbed him to the heart with his modeling-tool, and turned to Ferris and his friend. He slanted his broad red beard for a sidelong look at the picture, and said: "I know what you mean, Ferris. It's hard, and it's feeble in some ways and it looks a little too much like experimenting. But it isn't so *infernally* bad."

"Don't be fulsome," responded Ferris, jadedly. He was thinking in a thoroughly vanquished mood what a tragico-comic end of the whole business it was that poor Don Ippolito should come to his rescue in this fashion, and as it were offer to succor him in his extremity. He perceived the shamefulness of suffering such help; it would be much better to starve; but he felt cowed, and he had not courage to take arms against this sarcastic destiny, which had pursued him with a mocking smile from one lower level to another. He rubbed his forehead and brooded upon the picture. At least it would be some comfort to be rid of it; and Don Ippolito was dead; and to whom could it mean more than the face of it?

His friend had his way about framing it, and it was got into the exhibition. The hanging-committee offered it the hospi-talities of an obscure corner; but it was there, and it stood its chance. Nobody seemed to know that it was there, however, unless confronted with it by Ferris's friend, and then no one seemed to care for it, much less want to buy it. Ferris saw so many much worse pictures sold all around it, that he began gloomily to respect it. At first it had shocked him to see it on the Academy's wall; but it soon came to have no other relation to him than that of creatureship, like a poem in which a poet celebrates his love or laments his dead, and sells for a price. His pride as well as his poverty was set on having the picture sold; he had nothing to do, and he used to lurk about, and see if it would not interest somebody at last. But it remained unsold throughout May, and well into June, long after the crowds had ceased to frequent the exhibition, and only chance visitors from the country straggled in by twos and threes.

One warm, dusty afternoon, when he turned into the Academy out of Fourth Avenue, the empty hall echoed to no

W. D. Howells

footfall but his own. A group of weary women, who wore that look of wanting lunch which characterizes all picture-gallery-goers at home and abroad, stood faint before a certain large Venetian subject which Ferris abhorred, and the very name of which he spat out of his mouth with loathing for its unreality. He passed them with a sombre glance, as he took his way toward the retired spot where his own painting hung.

A lady whose crapes would have betrayed to her own sex the latest touch of Paris stood a little way back from it, and gazed fixedly at it. The pose of her head, her whole attitude, expressed a quiet dejection; without seeing her face one could know its air of pensive wistfulness. Ferris resolved to indulge himself in a near approach to this unwonted spectacle of interest in his picture; at the sound of his steps the lady slowly turned a face of somewhat heavily molded beauty, and from low-growing, thick pale hair and level brows, stared at him with the sad eyes of Florida Vervain. She looked fully the last two years older.

As though she were listening to the sound of his steps in the dark instead of having him there visibly before her, she kept her eyes upon him with a dreamy unrecognition.

"Yes, it is I," said Ferris, as if she had spoken.

She recovered herself, and with a subdued, sorrowful quiet in her old directness, she answered, "I supposed you must be in New York," and she indicated that she had supposed so from seeing this picture.

Ferris felt the blood mounting to his head. "Do you think it is like?" he asked.

"No," she said, "it isn't just to him; it attributes things that didn't belong to him, and it leaves out a great deal."

"I could scarcely have hoped to please you in a portrait of Don Ippolito." Ferris saw the red light break out as it used on the girl's pale cheeks, and her eyes dilate angrily. He went on recklessly: "He sent for me after you went away, and gave me a message for you. I never promised to deliver it, but I will do so now. He asked me to tell you when we met, that he had acted on your desire, and had tried to reconcile himself to his calling and his religion; he was going to enter a Carmelite convent."

Florida made no answer, but she seemed to expect him to go on, and he was constrained to do so.

"He never carried out his purpose," Ferris said, with a keen glance at her; "he died the night after I saw him."

"Died?" The fan and the parasol and the two or three light packages she had been holding slid down one by one, and lay at her feet. "Thank you for bringing me his last words," she said, but did not ask him anything more.

Ferris did not offer to gather up her things; he stood irresolute; presently he continued with a downcast look: "He had had a fever, but they thought he was getting well. His death must have been sudden." He stopped, and resumed fiercely, resolved to have the worst out: "I went to him, with no good-will toward him, the next day after I saw him; but I came too late. That was God's mercy to me. I hope you have your consolation, Miss Vervain."

It maddened him to see her so little moved, and he meant to make her share his remorse.

"Did he blame me for anything?" she asked.

"No!" said Ferris, with a bitter laugh, "he praised you."

"I am glad of that," returned Florida, "for I have thought it all over many times, and I know that I was not to blame, though at first I blamed myself. I never intended him anything but good. That is *my* consolation, Mr. Ferris. But you," she added, "you seem to make yourself my judge. Well, and what do *you* blame me for? I have a right to know what is in your mind."

The thing that was in his mind had rankled there for two years; in many a black reverie of those that alternated with his moods of abject self-reproach and perfect trust of her, he had confronted her and flung it out upon her in one stinging phrase. But he was now suddenly at a loss; the words would not come; his torment fell dumb before her; in her presence the cause was unspeakable. Her lips had quivered a little in making that demand, and there had been a corresponding break in her voice.

"Florida! Florida!" Ferris heard himself saying, "I loved you all the time!"

"Oh indeed, did you love me?" she cried, indignantly, while the tears shone in her eyes. "And was that why you left a helpless young girl to meet that trouble alone? Was that why you refused me your advice, and turned your back on me, and snubbed me? Oh, many thanks for your love!" She dashed the gathered tears angrily away, and went on. "Perhaps you knew, too, what that poor priest was thinking of?"

"Yes," said Ferris, stolidly, "I did at last: he told me."

"Oh, then you acted generously and nobly to let him go on! It was kind to him, and very, very kind to me!"

"What could I do?" demanded Ferris, amazed and furious to find himself on the defensive. "His telling me put it out of my power to act."

"I'm glad that you can satisfy yourself with such a quibble! But I wonder that you can tell *me*—*any* woman of it!"

"By Heavens, this is atrocious!" cried Ferris. "Do you think ... Look here!" he went on rudely. "I'll put the case to you, and you shall judge it. Remember that I was such a fool as to be in love with you. Suppose Don Ippolito had told me that he was going to risk everything—going to give up home, religion, friends—on the ten thousandth part of a chance that you might some day care for him. I did not believe he had even so much chance as that; but he had always thought me his friend, and he trusted me. Was it a quibble that kept me from betraying him? I don't know what honor is among women; but no *man* could have done it. I confess to my shame that I went to your house that night longing to betray him. And then suppose your mother sent me into the garden to call you, and I saw ... what has made my life a hell of doubt for the last two years; what ... No, excuse me! I can't put the case to you after all."

"What do you mean?" asked Florida. "I don't understand you!"

"What do I mean? You don't understand? Are you so blind as that, or are you making a fool of me? What could I think but that you had played with that priest's heart till your own"....

"Oh!" cried Florida with a shudder, starting away from him, "did you think I was such a wicked girl as that?"

It was no defense, no explanation, no denial; it simply left the case with Ferris as before. He stood looking like a man who does not know whether to bless or curse himself, to laugh or blaspheme.

She stooped and tried to pick up the things she had let fall upon the floor; but she seemed not able to find them. He bent over, and, gathering them together, returned them to her with his left hand, keeping the other in the breast of his coat.

"Thanks," she said; and then after a moment, "Have you been hurt?" she asked timidly.

"Yes," said Ferris in a sulky way. "I have had my share." He glanced down at his arm askance. "It's rather conventional," he added. "It isn't much of a hurt; but then, I wasn't much of a soldier."

The girl's eyes looked reverently at the conventional arm; those were the days, so long past, when women worshipped men for such things. But she said nothing, and as Ferris's eyes wandered to her, he received a novel and painful impression. He said, hesitatingly, "I have not asked before: but your mother, Miss Vervain—I hope she is well?"

"She is dead," answered Florida, with stony quiet.

They were both silent for a time. Then Ferris said, "I had a great affection for your mother."

"Yes," said the girl, "she was fond of you, too. But you never wrote or sent her any word; it used to grieve her."

Her unjust reproach went to his heart, so long preoccupied with its own troubles; he recalled with a tender remorse the old Venetian days and the kindliness of the gracious, silly woman who had seemed to like him so much; he remembered the charm of her perfect ladylikeness, and of her winning, weak-headed desire to make every one happy to whom she spoke; the beauty of the good-will, the hospitable soul that in an imaginably better world than this will outvalue a merely intellectual or aesthetic life. He humbled himself before her memory, and as keenly reproached himself as if he could have made her hear from him at any time during the past two years. He could only say, "I am sorry that I gave your mother pain; I loved her very truly. I hope that she did not suffer much before"—

"No," said Florida, "it was a peaceful end; but finally it was very sudden. She had not been well for many years, with that sort of decline; I used sometimes to feel troubled about her before we came to Venice; but I was very young. I never was really alarmed till that day I went to you."

"I remember," said Ferris contritely.

"She had fainted, and I thought we ought to see a doctor; but afterwards, because I thought that I ought not to do so without speaking to her, I did not go to the doctor; and that day we made up our minds to get home as soon as we could; and she seemed so much better, for a while; and then, everything seemed to happen at once. When we did start home, she could not go any farther than Switzerland, and in the fall we went back to Italy. We went to Sorrento, where the climate seemed to do her good. But she was growing frailer, the whole time. She died in March. I found some old friends of hers in Naples, and came home with them."

The girl hesitated a little over the words, which she nevertheless uttered unbroken, while the tears fell quietly down her face. She seemed to have forgotten the angry words that had passed between her and Ferris, to remember him only as one who had known her mother, while she went on to relate some little facts in the history of her mother's last days; and she rose into a higher, serener atmosphere, inaccessible to his resentment or his regret, as she spoke of her loss. The simple tale of sickness and death inexpressibly belittled his passionate woes, and made them look theatrical to him. He hung his head as they turned at her motion and walked away from the picture of Don Ippolito, and down the stairs toward the street-door; the people before the other Venetian picture had apparently yielded to their craving for lunch, and had vanished.

"I have very little to tell you of my own life," Ferris began awkwardly. "I came home soon after you started, and I went to Providence to find you, but you had not got back."

Florida stopped him and looked perplexedly into his face, and then moved on.

"Then I went into the army. I wrote once to you."

"I never got your letter," she said.

They were now in the lower hall, and near the door.

"Florida," said Ferris, abruptly, "I'm poor and disabled; I've no more right than any sick beggar in the street to say it to you; but I loved you, I must always love you. I—Good-by!"

She halted him again, and "You said," she grieved, "that you doubted me; you said that I had made your life a"—

"Yes, I said that; I know it," answered Ferris.

"You thought I could be such a false and cruel girl as that!"

"Yes, yes: I thought it all, God help me!"

"When I was only sorry for him, when it was you that I"—

"Oh, I know it," answered Ferris in a heartsick, hopeless voice. "He knew it, too. He told me so the day before he died."

"And didn't you believe him?"

Ferris could not answer.

"Do you believe him now?"

"I believe anything you tell me. When I look at you, I can't believe I ever doubted you."

"Why?"

"Because—because—I love you."

"Oh! That's no reason."

"I know it; but I'm used to being without a reason."

Florida looked gravely at his penitent face, and a brave red color mantled her own, while she advanced an unanswerable argument: "Then what are you going away for?"

The world seemed to melt and float away from between them. It returned and solidified at the sound of the janitor's steps as he came towards them on his round through the empty building. Ferris caught her hand; she leaned heavily upon his arm as they walked out into the street. It was all they could do at the moment except to look into each other's faces, and walk swiftly on.

At last, after how long a time he did not know, Ferris cried:

W. D. Howells

"Where are we going, Florida?"

"Why, I don't know!" she replied. "I'm stopping with those friends of ours at the Fifth Avenue Hotel. We *were* going on to Providence to-morrow. We landed yesterday; and we stayed to do some shopping"—

"And may I ask why you happened to give your first moments in America to the fine arts?"

"The fine arts? Oh! I thought I might find something of yours, there!"

At the hotel she presented him to her party as a friend whom her mother and she had known in Italy; and then went to lay aside her hat. The Providence people received him with the easy, half-southern warmth of manner which seems to have floated northward as far as their city on the Gulf Stream bathing the Rhode Island shores. The matron of the party had, before Florida came back, an outline history of their acquaintance, which she evolved from him with so much tact that he was not conscious of parting with information; and she divined indefinitely more when she saw them together again. She was charming; but to Ferris's thinking she had a fault, she kept him too much from Florida, though she talked of nothing else, and at the last she was discreetly merciful.

"Do you think," whispered Florida, very close against his face, when they parted, "that I'll have a bad temper?"

"I hope you will—or I shall be killed with kindness," he replied.

She stood a moment, nervously buttoning his coat across his breast. "You mustn't let that picture be sold, Henry," she said, and by this touch alone did she express any sense, if she had it, of his want of feeling in proposing to sell it. He winced, and she added with a soft pity in her voice, "He did bring us together, after all. I wish you had believed him, dear!"

"So do I," said Ferris, most humbly.

*   *   *   *   *

People are never equal to the romance of their youth in after life, except by fits, and Ferris especially could not keep himself at what he called the operatic pitch of their brief betrothal and the early days of their marriage. With his help, or even his encouragement, his wife might have been able to maintain it. She had a gift for idealizing him, at least, and as his hurt healed but slowly, and it was a good while before he could paint with his wounded arm, it was an easy matter for her to believe in the meanwhile that he would have been the greatest painter of his time, but for his honorable disability; to hear her, you would suppose no one else had ever been shot in the service of his country.

It was fortunate for Ferris, since he could not work, that she had money; in exalted moments he had thought this a barrier to their marriage; yet he could not recall any one who had refused the hand of a beautiful girl because of the accident of her wealth, and in the end he silenced his scruples. It might be said that in many other ways he was not her equal; but one ought to reflect how very few men are worthy of their wives in any sense. After his fashion he certainly loved her always,—even when she tried him most, for it must be owned that she really had that hot temper which he had dreaded in her from the first. Not that her imperiousness directly affected him. For a long time after their marriage, she seemed to have no other desire than to lose her outwearied will in his. There was something a little pathetic

W. D. Howells

in this; there was a kind of bewilderment in her gentleness, as though the relaxed tension of her long self-devotion to her mother left her without a full motive; she apparently found it impossible to give herself with a satisfactory degree of abandon to a man who could do so many things for himself. When her children came they filled this vacancy, and afforded her scope for the greatest excesses of self-devotion. Ferris laughed to find her protecting them and serving them with the same tigerish tenderness, the same haughty humility, as that with which she used to care for poor Mrs. Vervain; and he perceived that this was merely the direction away from herself of that intense arrogance of nature which, but for her power and need of loving, would have made her intolerable. What she chiefly exacted from them in return for her fierce devotedness was the truth in everything; she was content that they should be rather less fond of her than of their father, whom indeed they found much more amusing.

The Ferrises went to Europe some years after their marriage, revisiting Venice, but sojourning for the most part in Florence. Ferris had once imagined that the tragedy which had given him his wife would always invest her with the shadow of its sadness, but in this he was mistaken. There is nothing has really so strong a digestion as love, and this is very lucky, seeing what manifold experiences love has to swallow and assimilate; and when they got back to Venice, Ferris found that the customs of their joint life exorcised all the dark associations of the place. These simply formed a sombre background, against which their wedded happiness relieved itself. They talked much of the past, with free minds, unashamed and unafraid. If it is a little shocking, it is nevertheless true, and true to human nature, that they spoke of Don Ippolito as if he were a part of their love.

Ferris had never ceased to wonder at what he called the unfathomable innocence of his wife, and he liked to go over all the points of their former life in Venice, and bring home to himself the utter simplicity of her girlish ideas, motives, and designs, which both confounded and delighted him.

"It's amazing, Florida," he would say, "it's perfectly amazing that you should have been willing to undertake the job of importing into America that poor fellow with his whole stock of helplessness, dreamery, and unpracticality. What *were* you about?"

"Why, I've often told you, Henry. I thought he oughtn't to continue a priest."

"Yes, yes; I know." Then he would remain lost in thought, softly whistling to himself. On one of these occasions he asked, "Do you think he was really very much troubled by his false position?"

"I can't tell, now. He seemed to be so."

"That story he told you of his childhood and of how he became a priest; didn't it strike you at the time like rather a made-up, melodramatic history?"

"No, no! How can you say such things, Henry? It was too simple not to be true."

"Well, well. Perhaps so. But he baffles me. He always did, for that matter."

Then came another pause, while Ferris lay back upon the gondola cushions, getting the level of the Lido just under his hat-brim.

"Do you think he was very much of a skeptic, after all, Florida?"

Mrs. Ferris turned her eyes reproachfully upon her husband. "Why, Henry, how strange you are! You said yourself, once, that you used to wonder if he were not a skeptic."

"Yes; I know. But for a man who had lived in doubt so many years, he certainly slipped back into the bosom of mother church pretty suddenly. Don't you think he was a person of rather light feelings?"

"I can't talk with you, my dear, if you go on in that way."

"I don't mean any harm. I can see how in many things he was the soul of truth and honor. But it seems to me that even the life he lived was largely imagined. I mean that he was such a dreamer that once having fancied himself afflicted at being what he was, he could go on and suffer as keenly as if he really were troubled by it. Why mightn't it be that all his doubts came from anger and resentment towards those who made him a priest, rather than from any examination of his own mind? I don't say it *was* so. But I don't believe he knew quite what he wanted. He must have felt that his failure as an inventor went deeper than the failure of his particular attempts. I once thought that perhaps he had a genius in that way, but I question now whether he had. If he had, it seems to me he had opportunity to prove it—certainly, as a priest he had leisure to prove it. But when that sort of sub-consciousness of his own inadequacy came over him, it was perfectly natural for him to take refuge in the supposition that he had been baffled by circumstances."

Mrs. Ferris remained silently troubled. "I don't know how to answer you, Henry; but I think that you're judging him narrowly and harshly."

"Not harshly. I feel very compassionate towards him. But now, even as to what one might consider the most real thing in his life,—his caring for you,—it seems to me there must have been a great share of imagined sentiment in it. It was not a passion; it was a gentle nature's dream of a passion."

"He didn't die of a dream," said the wife.

"No, he died of a fever."

"He had got well of the fever."

"That's very true, my dear. And whatever his head was, he had an affectionate and faithful heart. I wish I had been gentler with him. I must often have bruised that sensitive soul. God knows I'm sorry for it. But he's a puzzle, he's a puzzle!"

Thus lapsing more and more into a mere problem as the years have passed, Don Ippolito has at last ceased to be even the memory of a man with a passionate love and a mortal sorrow. Perhaps this final effect in the mind of him who has realized the happiness of which the poor priest vainly dreamed is not the least tragic phase of the tragedy of Don Ippolito.

ABOUT THE AUTHOR

William Dean Howells (March 1, 1837 – May 11, 1920) was an American realist author and literary critic.

Born in Martins Ferry, Ohio, originally Martinsville, to William Cooper and Mary Dean Howells, Howells was the second of eight children. His father was a newspaper editor and printer, and the father moved frequently around Ohio. Howells began to help his father with typesetting and printing work at an early age. In 1852, his father arranged to have one of Howells' poems published in the Ohio State Journal without telling him.

He wrote his first novel, The Wedding Journey, in 1872, but his literary reputation took off with the realist novel, A Modern Instance, published in 1882, which described the decay of a marriage. His 1885 novel The Rise of Silas Lapham is perhaps his best known, describing the rise and fall of an American entrepreneur in the paint business. His social views were also strongly reflected in the novels Annie Kilburn (1888) and A Hazard of New Fortunes (1890). He was particularly outraged by the trials resulting from the Haymarket Riot.

In 1904, he was one of the first seven chosen for membership in the American Academy of Arts and Letters, of which he became president.

Choose from Thousands of 1stWorldLibrary Classics By

A. M. Barnard
Ada Leverson
Adolphus William Ward
Aesop
Agatha Christie
Alexander Aaronsohn
Alexander Kielland
Alexandre Dumas
Alfred Gatty
Alfred Ollivant
Alice Duer Miller
Alice Turner Curtis
Alice Dunbar
Allen Chapman
Alleyne Ireland
Ambrose Bierce
Amelia E. Barr
Amory H. Bradford
Andrew Lang
Andrew McFarland Davis
Andy Adams
Angela Brazil
Anna Alice Chapin
Anna Sewell
Annie Besant
Annie Hamilton Donnell
Annie Payson Call
Annie Roe Carr
Annonaymous
Anton Chekhov
Archibald Lee Fletcher
Arnold Bennett
Arthur C. Benson
Arthur Conan Doyle
Arthur M. Winfield
Arthur Ransome
Arthur Schnitzler
Arthur Train
Atticus
B.H. Baden-Powell
B. M. Bower
B. C. Chatterjee
Baroness Emmuska Orczy
Baroness Orczy
Basil King
Bayard Taylor
Ben Macomber
Bertha Muzzy Bower
Bjornstjerne Bjornson

Booth Tarkington
Boyd Cable
Bram Stoker
C. Collodi
C. E. Orr
C. M. Ingleby
Carolyn Wells
Catherine Parr Traill
Charles A. Eastman
Charles Amory Beach
Charles Dickens
Charles Dudley Warner
Charles Farrar Browne
Charles Ives
Charles Kingsley
Charles Klein
Charles Hanson Towne
Charles Lathrop Pack
Charles Romyn Dake
Charles Whibley
Charles Willing Beale
Charlotte M. Braeme
Charlotte M. Yonge
Charlotte Perkins Stetson
Clair W. Hayes
Clarence Day Jr.
Clarence E. Mulford
Clemence Housman
Confucius
Coningsby Dawson
Cornelis DeWitt Wilcox
Cyril Burleigh
D. H. Lawrence
Daniel Defoe
David Garnett
Dinah Craik
Don Carlos Janes
Donald Keyhoe
Dorothy Kilner
Dougan Clark
Douglas Fairbanks
E. Nesbit
E. P. Roe
E. Phillips Oppenheim
E. S. Brooks
Earl Barnes
Edgar Rice Burroughs
Edith Van Dyne
Edith Wharton

Edward Everett Hale
Edward J. O'Biren
Edward S. Ellis
Edwin L. Arnold
Eleanor Atkins
Eleanor Hallowell Abbott
Eliot Gregory
Elizabeth Gaskell
Elizabeth McCracken
Elizabeth Von Arnim
Ellem Key
Emerson Hough
Emilie F. Carlen
Emily Bronte
Emily Dickinson
Enid Bagnold
Enilor Macartney Lane
Erasmus W. Jones
Ernie Howard Pie
Ethel May Dell
Ethel Turner
Ethel Watts Mumford
Eugene Sue
Eugenie Foa
Eugene Wood
Eustace Hale Ball
Evelyn Everett-green
Everard Cotes
F. H. Cheley
F. J. Cross
F. Marion Crawford
Fannie E. Newberry
Federick Austin Ogg
Ferdinand Ossendowski
Fergus Hume
Florence A. Kilpatrick
Fremont B. Deering
Francis Bacon
Francis Darwin
Frances Hodgson Burnett
Frances Parkinson Keyes
Frank Gee Patchin
Frank Harris
Frank Jewett Mather
Frank L. Packard
Frank V. Webster
Frederic Stewart Isham
Frederick Trevor Hill
Frederick Winslow Taylor

Friedrich Kerst
Friedrich Nietzsche
Fyodor Dostoyevsky
G.A. Henty
G.K. Chesterton
Gabrielle E. Jackson
Garrett P. Serviss
Gaston Leroux
George A. Warren
George Ade
Geroge Bernard Shaw
George Cary Eggleston
George Durston
George Ebers
George Eliot
George Gissing
George MacDonald
George Meredith
George Orwell
George Sylvester Viereck
George Tucker
George W. Cable
George Wharton James
Gertrude Atherton
Gordon Casserly
Grace E. King
Grace Gallatin
Grace Greenwood
Grant Allen
Guillermo A. Sherwell
Gulielma Zollinger
Gustav Flaubert
H. A. Cody
H. B. Irving
H.C. Bailey
H. G. Wells
H. H. Munro
H. Irving Hancock
H. R. Naylor
H. Rider Haggard
H. W. C. Davis
Haldeman Julius
Hall Caine
Hamilton Wright Mabie
Hans Christian Andersen
Harold Avery
Harold McGrath
Harriet Beecher Stowe
Harry Castlemon
Harry Coghill
Harry Houidini

Hayden Carruth
Helent Hunt Jackson
Helen Nicolay
Hendrik Conscience
Hendy David Thoreau
Henri Barbusse
Henrik Ibsen
Henry Adams
Henry Ford
Henry Frost
Henry James
Henry Jones Ford
Henry Seton Merriman
Henry W Longfellow
Herbert A. Giles
Herbert Carter
Herbert N. Casson
Herman Hesse
Hildegard G. Frey
Homer
Honore De Balzac
Horace B. Day
Horace Walpole
Horatio Alger Jr.
Howard Pyle
Howard R. Garis
Hugh Lofting
Hugh Walpole
Humphry Ward
Ian Maclaren
Inez Haynes Gillmore
Irving Bacheller
Isabel Cecilia Williams
Isabel Hornibrook
Israel Abrahams
Ivan Turgenev
J.G.Austin
J. Henri Fabre
J. M. Barrie
J. M. Walsh
J. Macdonald Oxley
J. R. Miller
J. S. Fletcher
J. S. Knowles
J. Storer Clouston
J. W. Duffield
Jack London
Jacob Abbott
James Allen
James Andrews
James Baldwin

James Branch Cabell
James DeMille
James Joyce
James Lane Allen
James Lane Allen
James Oliver Curwood
James Oppenheim
James Otis
James R. Driscoll
Jane Abbott
Jane Austen
Jane L. Stewart
Janet Aldridge
Jens Peter Jacobsen
Jerome K. Jerome
Jessie Graham Flower
John Buchan
John Burroughs
John Cournos
John F. Kennedy
John Gay
John Glasworthy
John Habberton
John Joy Bell
John Kendrick Bangs
John Milton
John Philip Sousa
John Taintor Foote
Jonas Lauritz Idemil Lie
Jonathan Swift
Joseph A. Altsheler
Joseph Carey
Joseph Conrad
Joseph E. Badger Jr
Joseph Hergesheimer
Joseph Jacobs
Jules Vernes
Julian Hawthrone
Julie A Lippmann
Justin Huntly McCarthy
Kakuzo Okakura
Karle Wilson Baker
Kate Chopin
Kenneth Grahame
Kenneth McGaffey
Kate Langley Bosher
Kate Langley Bosher
Katherine Cecil Thurston
Katherine Stokes
L. A. Abbot
L. T. Meade

L. Frank Baum
Latta Griswold
Laura Dent Crane
Laura Lee Hope
Laurence Housman
Lawrence Beasley
Leo Tolstoy
Leonid Andreyev
Lewis Carroll
Lewis Sperry Chafer
Lilian Bell
Lloyd Osbourne
Louis Hughes
Louis Joseph Vance
Louis Tracy
Louisa May Alcott
Lucy Fitch Perkins
Lucy Maud Montgomery
Luther Benson
Lydia Miller Middleton
Lyndon Orr
M. Corvus
M. H. Adams
Margaret E. Sangster
Margret Howth
Margaret Vandercook
Margaret W. Hungerford
Margret Penrose
Maria Edgeworth
Maria Thompson Daviess
Mariano Azuela
Marion Polk Angellotti
Mark Overton
Mark Twain
Mary Austin
Mary Catherine Crowley
Mary Cole
Mary Hastings Bradley
Mary Roberts Rinehart
Mary Rowlandson
M. Wollstonecraft Shelley
Maud Lindsay
Max Beerbohm
Myra Kelly
Nathaniel Hawthrone
Nicolo Machiavelli
O. F. Walton
Oscar Wilde

Owen Johnson
P.G. Wodehouse
Paul and Mabel Thorne
Paul G. Tomlinson
Paul Severing
Percy Brebner
Percy Keese Fitzhugh
Peter B. Kyne
Plato
Quincy Allen
R. Derby Holmes
R. L. Stevenson
R. S. Ball
Rabindranath Tagore
Rahul Alvares
Ralph Bonehill
Ralph Henry Barbour
Ralph Victor
Ralph Waldo Emmerson
Rene Descartes
Ray Cummings
Rex Beach
Rex E. Beach
Richard Harding Davis
Richard Jefferies
Richard Le Gallienne
Robert Barr
Robert Frost
Robert Gordon Anderson
Robert L. Drake
Robert Lansing
Robert Lynd
Robert Michael Ballantyne
Robert W. Chambers
Rosa Nouchette Carey
Rudyard Kipling
Saint Augustine
Samuel B. Allison
Samuel Hopkins Adams
Sarah Bernhardt
Sarah C. Hallowell
Selma Lagerlof
Sherwood Anderson
Sigmund Freud
Standish O'Grady
Stanley Weyman
Stella Benson
Stella M. Francis

Stephen Crane
Stewart Edward White
Stijn Streuvels
Swami Abhedananda
Swami Parmananda
T. S. Ackland
T. S. Arthur
The Princess Der Ling
Thomas A. Janvier
Thomas A Kempis
Thomas Anderton
Thomas Bailey Aldrich
Thomas Bulfinch
Thomas De Quincey
Thomas Dixon
Thomas H. Huxley
Thomas Hardy
Thomas More
Thornton W. Burgess
U. S. Grant
Upton Sinclair
Valentine Williams
Various Authors
Vaughan Kester
Victor Appleton
Victor G. Durham
Victoria Cross
Virginia Woolf
Wadsworth Camp
Walter Camp
Walter Scott
Washington Irving
Wilbur Lawton
Wilkie Collins
Willa Cather
Willard F. Baker
William Dean Howells
William le Queux
W. Makepeace Thackeray
William W. Walter
William Shakespeare
Winston Churchill
Yei Theodora Ozaki
Yogi Ramacharaka
Young E. Allison
Zane Grey

www.ingramcontent.com/pod-product-compliance
Lightning Source LLC
Chambersburg PA
CBHW050037180626
46810CB00002B/766